To Iceland, With Love

I. C. Springman

DEDICATION

To the far-seeing and courageous People of Iceland
and to *Indignados* everywhere.

For DLW, SVP, and RWR
First, last, and always...

CONTENTS

BEFORE –
Burning Down the House

December 2008. A darkened conference room in McClean, Virginia. Above a semi-circle of motionless heads belonging to anonymous U.S. intelligence honchos, a Power Point presentation was in progress. The words "Operation Ghost Dance: Background" monopolized a wall-sized flat-screen TV.

Over an intercom, a dry and disembodied voice recounted the relevant facts. "On 15 September 2008, the U.S. Department of the Treasury suffered a significant information system breach. Sensitive data was compromised, much of it relating to the evolving global financial crisis."

The screen displayed side-by-side mug shots of a man and a woman – our heroes-to-be, John and Jane Doe.

"Subsequent investigation back-traced the perpetrator across the web with inconclusive results. However, further data analysis and mapping revealed a disturbing fact: two contract employees of two separate tier-one agencies –"

Here a house flashed on the screen – a two-story 1930's traditional in an affluent New York City bedroom community, say Scarsdale or New Rochelle. White clapboard siding and black shutters. Nice landscaping.

"—lived at the physical address associated with one of the so-called 'bounce points' or intermediate computers implicated in the breach.

Expedited inquiry confirmed intelligence community security guidelines were violated as follows--"

The screen filled with the words "Personal Conduct – Failure to Disclose."

"Both employees failed to disclose the potentially compromising nature of their relationship, which could be expected to have consequences for sensitive compartmented information. While their marriage of approximately six years duration was known –"

Close-up of wedding photo. A tuxedoed John and a radiant white-gowned Jane locked in a passionate post-ceremony embrace.

"—neither agency was properly briefed as to spousal vocation, raising fundamental questions of judgment, lack of candor, reliability, and trust."

The screen filled with the words "Psychological Considerations – Failure to Report."

"Both employees failed to report that they entered marital counseling a brief time ago, nor did they seek the services of agency-certified therapists as required."

The words "Financial Considerations – Debt-to-Income Ratio" took center screen.

"Both employees moved from direct tier-one employment to contract status circa 2005, possibly lured by the prospect of higher private sector earnings. In 2007, the Continuous Competitiveness model implemented by the Department of Homeland Security reduced net income service-wide."

The screen now showed a graph with a green income line trending down and an orange debt line trending up, with a red arrow measuring the 125% gap in between.

"Apparently, the couple failed to adjust in a timely manner. When these issues came to light, their debt-to-income ratio exceeded agency standards by a considerable margin."

The screen flipped again, displaying the words "Handling Protected Information – Risk Management Violations."

"Though all branches of the U.S. Intelligence community have a common mission and set of interests, segmentation of information is an accepted operational necessity. The potential for breach of client confidentiality, negligent disclosure of proprietary knowledge, or other unauthorized release of sensitive protected information is greatly magnified by personal relationships."

A photo from Pearl Harbor, with battleship sinking amid smoke and flames, fleetingly illustrated the moderator's point.

"Basic risk assessment and management practices required that both employees notify supervisors of close daily contact with intelligence agents responsible to another chain of command. This did not occur."

The words "Information Technology Systems – Illegal or Unauthorized Use" appeared. The moderator took a sip of water, which went down the wrong way. He coughed. His bored audience shifted impatiently. He went on.

"Illegal or unauthorized entry into any information technology system; illegal or unauthorized modification, destruction, manipulation, or denial of access to information, software, firmware, or hardware in an information technology system; downloading, storing, or transmitting information on or to any unauthorized software, hardware, or information technology system is strictly prohibited."

The accompanying cartoon of a spy in a fake Groucho Marx nose, kneeling beside a filing cabinet and transferring files marked 'TOP SECRET' and 'CONFIDENTIAL' into a briefcase, seemed to aggravate the audience even further. There were vague mutterings. The moderator pressed doggedly forward.

"Data accessed in the 15 September Treasury breach was routed through a device physically located in the couple's residence. No satisfactory explanation for this eventuality has emerged nor has the couple volunteered exculpatory information."

The screen filled with one very large word: "COMPLICATIONS." The mutterings ceased. The moderator cleared his throat.

"Network forensics tie the 15 September breach to prior and subsequent incursions of equal or greater sensitivity at the Departments of Defense and State, SWIFT interbank transfer system, and the World Bank. The potential for harm to national security, key allies, and global stability cannot be overstated."

Another split-screen now displayed John and Jane in full battle rattle in separate combat situations.

"Employees are National Clandestine Service Paramilitary Operations Officers – Delta Force and Special Activities Division."

A new electricity filled the air. Several of the bigwigs sat forward in their seats. The word "TIMELINE" flashed up, and as the moderator spoke, a series of dates appeared.

"On 25 September a Joint DIA/CIA task force was formed: Operation Ghost Dance. As of 28 September, Test One commenced. Blanket surveillance was initiated and employees (hereafter 'targets') were separately assigned the same mission –

Briefly, a wanted poster displayed, the picture of a wide-eyed and wooly-headed young man with a bulls-eye superimposed over his guileless face.

"—a decoy assassination. Both failed, a notable anomaly given their combined career kill rates of above 97.5%. Both claimed failure was due to 'circumstances beyond their control.' On 30 September, Test Two commenced. Targets were assigned to assassinate each other. It was expected they would a) confess or b) flee. The assignment deadline passed without result—"

The screen exhibited a picture of John and Jane's lovely house engulfed in flames and surrounded by a SWAT team.

"—at which point a SWAT team was dispatched to the targets' place of residence with orders to apprehend and detain. Targets resisted with deadly force. Residence caught fire, several assets were liquidated, and targets fled in a neighbor's minivan."

Photo of a minivan pursued by multiple cars and SUVs, guns blazing in both directions. Background collisions and rollovers of both civilian and pursuit vehicles added to the sense of mayhem.

"A high-speed chase ensued, during which several agency vehicles were totaled and several more assets liquidated."

Photo of a convention center advertising a Home and Garden Expo. It was night, the parking lot deserted.

"Targets were eventually cornered after hours at a Home and Garden Show."

Photo of absolute carnage. A convention center packed with vendor booths dedicated to fencing, siding, flooring, kitchen and bath products, home furnishings, lawn care, and DIY projects riddled with bullet holes and festooned with lifeless bodies.

"A gun battle resulted in the loss of an additional sixteen assets, giving us a final score of: targets - two dozen, home team - zero. And the targets escaped. At which point they were added to the domestic Joint Prioritized Effect List. Capture or kill."

One final screen, one final word: "STATUS."

"Targets' last confirmed location was La Paz, Mexico. Current whereabouts unknown."

The screen faded to black. A door opened in one corner of the room, and most of the honchos rose silently and drifted, like so many spirits of the damned, toward the gray light of the hallway. Two heads remained. Once the room was clear, the fireworks began.

Head #1: "What the fuck?! If this shit ever hits the fan –"

Head #2: "Nobody can connect that many dots."

Head #1: "The fuck you say."

Head #2: "The fuck I say. And if they did, who's going to believe it?"

I. C. SPRINGMAN

1 ONCE IN A LIFETIME

They were lucky to get out with their skins. They were alive, they had each other, and that was about it. Plenty of nothing – and the boat.

A sleek and agile sloop, about thirty feet, painted black. At that particular moment in the history of the world she was riding gently at anchor off the coast of Cayo Largo. Turquoise waters that seemed to stretch all the way to Mexico underlined the flowing white script of her name. Not that there was anyone to admire her or read what was written on her hull; all the nudists had gone back to their nice warm hotels for the evening. And reading is a dying art aboard this dying planet anyway. But, for the record, the one word scrawled across her oil-dark flank was 'Casablanca.'

She was headed into the sunset, a show that went on despite the absence of audience. Plum and coral clouds rippled from horizon to horizon like cheap ostrich plumes. Behind them, the bawdy old sun finished up her fan dance and left the stage in a naked blaze of every worn out cliché you can think of. A flock of vagrant seabirds dropped by for a nightcap and fell asleep right there on the rocking face of the deep, like so many drunks in a strip joint. The party was definitely over. In the cockpit of the sailboat, someone had shoved a champagne bottle head first into a battered silver ice bucket. The deck was otherwise deserted, the sails furled for the day. Somewhere some cosmic stagehand threw a switch and the shivering curtain of night descended.

Down below, the teak-lined cabin rated comparison with an antique jewelry box. Or a really nice casket. Lots of highly polished wood and

I. C. SPRINGMAN

brass fittings.   There was a double berth forward, wedged into the triangle of the bow.   The galley and head were aft, while the main salon with its beige upholstered benches and drop-leaf table occupied the midship.   To one side of the salon, near a desk with a built-in two-way radio, two tall, ridiculously attractive people held champagne flutes and each other.   In the tiny available space, they were slow-dancing.   Or perhaps just swaying with the rise and fall of the waves:

Let's fall in love, why shouldn't we fall in love?

Our hearts are made of it, let's take a chance, why be afraid of it?

"Ahoy there, you two.   It's been awhile."   Reluctantly, the dancers unwound from one another and turned to face a computer open on the desktop.   Not too terribly far away in the Caymen Islands, their mild-mannered accountant could be seen sipping a glass of sherry in his posh office.   Behind him rose shelves stuffed to the breaking point with legal and accounting tomes.   The jovial Gerald, his craggy face topped with a shock of white hair, spoke in the clipped tones of an upper crust Brit. "Tired of playing Pirates of the Caribbean yet?"

John looked at Jane, who was entirely fetching in jeans and a rough-knit fisherman's sweater.   In his mind's eye he exchanged the sweater for a lacy pirate's shirt and the jeans for thigh-high leather boots.   "Now there's a little idea, matey."

Jane gave John her best one-eyed pirate leer.   "Yarrr, swash-buckle our way up around the Hamptons, maybe."   She reached up to stroke his cheek, which was covered with stubble, razor blades being one of the items they were currently rationing.   "You could definitely give Blackbeard a run for his money."

"Well, you'd best do something, and quick, dear boy," Gerald advised.   "I'm about to cash out your BP position and after that you'll be running very nearly on empty.   Which, as I warned you often enough, is what comes of spendthrift ways--"

"And not saving for retirement or a rainy day."   Jane finished his sentence for him, hectoring tone and all.   "Blaming the victim, you know.   We got shafted in the defined contribution changeover?   Also the house was supposed to be an investment.   And let's not forget that little

8

financial crisis thing last fall," Jane pushed her long dark hair behind one ear. "A third of everything – poof." She waved her champagne flute like a magic wand.

"We hear you, Gerry. We're scraping bottom. But you know how we're situated. Just give it to us straight," John said, putting an arm around Jane's waist and squeezing to signal that they needed to focus on the matter at hand.

"Right," Jane chimed in with unwonted meekness, "how long have we got?" She reached up and gave John's nascent beard a sly yank.

"Ow!" John complained and pretended to bite the hand that hurt him.

"Chin up, children," Gerald tried to sound encouraging as he put down the sherry to don a pair of horn-rimmed glasses. He surveyed with a perplexed air the broad and cluttered expanse of his desk. "Given that it's black days all around, you're actually doing better than most. Which should tell you something. Your homeowner's insurance paid off the mortgage. Of course your neighbors wish you'd do something about the smoking ruins, but half of them are under water and looking at foreclosure, so I wouldn't let it keep me up nights. Ah!" Having pawed through a pile of nearly identical folders, he selected one, opened it, and ran a finger down a ledger sheet affixed to the left flap.

Jane made a mournful little sound. "I miss the house."

John bent to kiss her neck. "Different world." Then, feeling he still hadn't gotten the answer he needed, he persisted. "So? How far are we from absolute zero? Three months? Six?"

"More like two," Gerald admitted reluctantly. "If you're lucky. And stop spending money entirely. No more *pain au chocolat* shipped to Costa Rica from," he squinted to make out an entry on the ledger sheet, "Patisserie Claude, for heaven's sake."

"It was our anniversary," Jane pouted. "We always have breakfast at Claude's on our anniversary."

"And dinner at Le Meurice," John added.

"Le Meurice. In Paris? That Le Meurice?" Gerald asked.

"Standing reservation," John affirmed.

"Ooh, you know? We forgot to cancel," Jane winced. "But naturally, since we couldn't fly to France, the least we could do was -"

"Have French pastries flown in from New York. Naturally," Gerald agreed drily.

"I thought we were being downright frugal," Jane insisted. "And we did buy American."

Gerald looked down his nose. "Judging from what they cost, *pain d'or* would be closer to the mark. I'd advise you to avoid nostalgia for the nonce. You can't afford it. At least till you manage to reinvigorate the old cash flow. Where are you, by the by?" Gerald put down his eyeglasses and reclaimed his glass of sherry.

"Wrong side of Cuba," John said.

"I'll wire what's left to Havana, then." Gerald lifted his glass in a toast. "Cheerio, pip-pip!"

"Cheerio," Jane echoed half-heartedly, lifting her empty glass.

John groaned, dropped onto one of the benches, and flopped over sideways. "OK. That's that. Honeymoon's over. Again."

Jane sat down next to him and removed his champagne flute to safety. "Cheer up."

"Oh right. It's only money. Was that the last bottle of champagne, by the way?"

"Now, now. Tell you what. If all else fails – and nobody kills us," she was careful to stipulate, "I'll buy you a parrot."

"We're too broke to buy a parrot," John maintained dolefully.

Jane reached into the bookshelf above him and pulled out a slightly dog-eared copy of the Wall Street Journal. "Ah-ah-ah! It's capital equipment. No pirate ship can be expected to operate without one. Under new depreciation rules we can write off the entire cost" she paused to consult the relevant article, "year one."

"Yo-ho-ho!" John grabbed her and pulled her down on top of him, newspaper and all. "Anything in there about a bottle of rum? On second thought, you better make it a case."

2 ROAD TO NOWHERE

It was a twenty-minute trip from Marina Hemingway to Old Havana. They had trouble boarding the only local transport option, a cross between a tractor-trailer and a bus known as '*el camello*' – 'the camel.' It was already bursting at the seams with overheated, long-suffering Cubans. Jane stopped short, though the driver smiled and beckoned them forward.

"Problem?" John looked from Jane, in her simple black shift dress and ballet flats, to the ramshackle conveyance.

"Pink." Jane shuddered. "Why'd it have to be pink?" She was correct. Underneath about a decade of dust and poorly expunged graffiti, the camel sported an industrial grade coat of princess pink. "*BCD?*" she asked the driver, indicating the graffiti.

"Bajo condiciones difíciles. Dos dolares, por favor, senor, senora."

"'Under difficult conditions.' That's not graffiti, that's truth in advertising." Jane shook her head at the driver. *"Pero, no hay sitio en el autobus."*

John had to agree. "It's pretty crowded."

The driver looked at them with patient pity and used his hands British butler fashion to herd them toward the open door. *"Senora. Senor. Por favor."*

Ushering Jane to the steps of the vehicle, he smacked the backside of the last rider to board. *"Apartado, el gordo."* If the rider thus assaulted was not amused, those in front of him were even less so. Many curses and much grumbling ensued, mostly *sotto voce*, but in the end the bottom step was cleared for Jane and two pullman-style carryalls. Not for the first time, Jane found herself forced to acknowledge the existence of a higher power – in this case that of Cuban ingenuity in the face of dollar-bearing *yanquis*. But their problem was only half solved.

"Coming?" Jane said half archly, half challengingly to John, who was still stuck in pedestrian class. The driver beckoned again, as though coaxing a very small child.

"No way," John protested.

"Si," the driver insisted flatly. "Way. *La senora es muy bonita. Y son ustedes casados, no?"* ("The lady is very pretty. And you are married, right?") Obediently, John clambered up and, after a brief interlude of grunting and exertion on the part of the driver and conjugal hilarity on the part of John and Jane, the doors were forced shut and the camel set off. In a spume of thick black diesel exhaust. Slouching toward *la Habana Vieja*.

3 BRAND NEW DAY

The camel came to a snorting, choking halt under a palm tree in la Plaza de Armas. Almost before the doors opened, impatient, half-suffocated passengers exploded from every possible exit, including the windows. Not expecting so much kinetic energy from such a listless crowd, John pitched backward toward the curb. Jane managed to swing from a handrail to relative safety, but the luggage went tumbling end over end, aided by a few well-placed kicks from exasperated locals. Like salmon swimming upstream, a fresh horde of weary sweating Cubans, frantic to occupy even so much as a sardine's space in the pink tin can, fought to get onboard, unintentionally blocking the outflow of those equally frantic to disembark.

"Thanks. What? Hey!" John lunged for one of the bags as an enterprising young Cuban in a pair of American sneakers only a year or two out of fashion prepared to expropriate it. A minor tug-of-war ensued. Jane made a beeline for the remaining carryall, trusting John to handle the situation with minimal bloodshed and without sparking an international incident. Turning back, she was surprised to find that John had been preempted, and that his hapless tourist cover remained intact. The driver of the camel, risking the wrath of his unadoring public by deferring departure, had climbed down from his cab and trotted the entire length of the eighteen-wheeler to intervene. He spoke to the youth in terse and ironic disapproval: *"Es siempre el cerdo capitalista que mata el ganso de oro."* ("It is always the capitalist pig who kills the golden goose.")

The youth shrugged, *"Los cerdos están ganando, cabron."* ("The pigs are winning, asshole.")

"No en Cuba, menso. Vaya a casa y no diré a su madre. O la guardia. ("Not in Cuba, smartass. Go home and I won't tell your mother. Or the neighborhood watch.") He watched the kid jog away toward an impromptu soccer match and shook his head. *"En esas manos la revolución. Dios nos ayuda."* ("In those hands the revolution. God help us.") He touched two fingers to his Chicago Cubs baseball cap and turned away, playfully shaking his fist at his passengers, who had been beseeching him and cursing him in equal measure the entire time.

"Muchas gracias," John hastened to call after him. "Can you recommend a good hotel?" The driver turned back willingly.

"El Hotel Sevilla en el Paseo del Prado. Es el hotel mas fina de la Habana. Una vez que fui alli." (The Sevilla Hotel in Prado Street. It is the finest hotel in Havana. Once upon a time I went there.") He smiled, remembering the luxurious accommodations awaiting them – the Moorish architecture, the antique furnishings, the marble bathrooms, and on the bed rose petals and thick towels twisted in the shape of a swan...

Jane and John exchanged a glance. It was Jane who spoke, somewhat reluctantly: *"Por favor, hay un buen hotel de la economia cerca aqui? Quiza un Motel del Ocho?"* ("Is there a good economy hotel nearby? A Motel 8 maybe?")

The driver looked at them sideways a moment. *"Si, si. Alrededor de la esquina. El edificio con los obturadores azules. Está donde aqui las alemanes del este usados para ir."* He pointed and smiled wryly. ("Around the corner. The building with the blue shutters. That is where the East Germans used to go.")

"Oh great. We're not only not in Kansas anymore, Toto, we're not even in the First World," Jane muttered. "I liked slumming a whole lot better when it wasn't a lifestyle."

"Let's review. First World equals money, yes, AND former colleagues who get bonus points for bumping us off. Third World equals poverty and who the hell are you, *gringo*?" John offered a folded bill to the driver, who stepped back, bowed, and said in perfect English: "Our poverty comes in large part from your unending embargo, *mis amigos.*

15

And we are but a tiny example in the world you run. *Muchas gracias* and welcome to Cuba. *Senor. Senora.*"

The rebuke came as something of a shock. Like the murder in Camus's *L'Etranger* - on sale nearby at one of the many second-hand bookstalls for which the Plaza was famous - it was unexpected and inexplicable. For about five seconds. For about five seconds the world froze. Nothing and nobody moved. Then someone somewhere clicked the cosmic 'Resume' button. The sun crashed down with unseasonal ferocity, street musicians overdubbed one another with earsplitting intensity, and a passive-aggressive mule stuck between the shafts of a vegetable cart dropped a fresh and pungent load of manure on cobblestones a street sweeper had just rinsed clean.

Conscious of the neon sign flashing over her head – 'UGLY AMERICAN! UGLY AMERICAN! - Jane looked from John to the mule and back again. "Even he knows I'm an ass."

John gave her a friendly nudge. "Everybody's a critic. But we should definitely be punished. You must give us all a good spanking," he teased. They were trundling along the Calle Obispo now, where everything - from the baroque buildings left over from colonial days to the highly polished vintage automobiles to the tilting towers of the two hundred year old cathedral - was beautiful and falling apart. They turned the corner to find a flock of paper birds fluttering from a network of strings stretching from rooftop to rooftop all the way down the block and beyond. Jane eyed the only house with blue shutters. "Oh, no worries on the punishment front. I'd say we're already in line for a lot of what we have coming."

It was a squat two-story structure that looked to be suffering from some disease, a skin disorder that had left the exterior blotchy and caused stucco to peel away in sizable patches. Someone had applied a coat of whitewash in a half-hearted attempt to smooth things over, but the effort was negated by the tall blue shutters, which were only partially painted, as though either the paint or the painter's good intentions had run out about halfway through. Delicate ironwork fenced the second floor balcony, where the day's laundry twisted and floated like so many angels restrained by wooden clothespins. A child's crib stood at one end, drafted into service as a container garden and densely overgrown with baby banana trees, mint, and tomato plants in bloom. Flowering jasmine vines curled up over the roof and down to the street. In the middle of the building on the first floor, a pair of narrow wooden doors opened into the hotel lobby. In a spirit of resigned foreboding, they entered.

So strongly did the desk clerk resemble the driver of the camel (minus the Cub's cap), that John and Jane stared at him very hard for a long moment before speaking.

"May I help you?" the desk clerk inquired, but in a tone that suggested he would prefer not to do anything of the sort.

"We'd like to check in," John said.

"Do you have a reservation?" The desk clerk gave the impression that he sincerely doubted it.

"No, 'fraid not. We're just betting the farm that there's room at the inn." The old-fashioned cubby behind the front desk had a key dangling from every square, making this a pretty safe gamble. But the desk clerk was not amused.

"That hasn't always worked out so well. However today is your lucky day. Passports?" John handed them over. "Americans. Huh."

John did not look up from the old-fashioned hotel register that he was signing. "You were saying?"

"Usted era érase una vez rico y estúpido," the desk clerk stated bluntly, in Spanish. ("Once upon a time you were rich and stupid.")

"Y ahora?" Jane asked, leaning one elbow on the massive front desk. The desk clerk bowed slightly, as if knowing his language earned them a grudging sort of entry-level respect. He reverted to English.

"Not rich or you wouldn't be here. The good news? Being *socialistas* we only put bedbugs in our very best hotels." He handed John a key and pointed to the stairs. "The elevator has been out of order since 1992."

"Hear that, honey?" John said in his best southern drawl, "No bedbugs."

"JP Morgan has bedbugs – I read that somewhere," Jane commented, eying and scrupulously not touching the banister.

"What I want to know is – when did we stop being the good guys?" John surveyed a short dim hallway, trying to make out the room numbers. "You know he gave us 13?"

"What you mean we, Paleface. Or was that a trick question?"

John bent to unlock the door, which, despite being as flimsy as a piece of cardboard, refused to open, resisting repeated attempts to insert and turn the key. He rattled the knob and the door threatened to come off its rusty hinges. "Is this a trick door?" He stepped back in frustration. The door swung open of its own accord. John and Jane stared mutely and with frozen faces at the cracked turquoise walls, the sharp-edged wrought-iron bed, the hole near the window where the air conditioner should have been.

"Pretty basic," John allowed.

"I have to take issue with your use of the word 'pretty,' Jane replied tartly.

John took her bag from her and stepped over the threshold. *"Somos todos los cubanos ahora, carina."* ("We're all Cubans now, darlin'.")

4 NOBODY TOLD ME

After not taking a shower in the turquoise-tiled bathroom - Jane having found an economy-sized cockroach doing the backstroke in the rust-stained tub - they decided to go in search of *mojitos*, the Cuban drink of legend.

"Let me guess," the desk clerk said as they came downstairs. He sat slouched behind the fortress of the front desk, book in hand. "You want to know where to get the best *mojito*. You want to drink where Hemingway drank." He rose and laid the book on the desktop, face down and spread-eagled so they could read the title: "The Post-American World."

"Don't give him the satisfaction," Jane muttered, pretending to brush a hair or cabbage leaf off John's shoulder.

"Don't be ridiculous," John muttered back, slipping his arm around her. "Actually we were wondering where we should go to eat."

"The closest McDonald's is about 500 miles away. In Guantanamo," the desk clerk said, his face bland and helpful.

"Gee, I don't know, that sounds like quite a hike. Nothing in the neighborhood, then? Communism and cooking don't mix, I guess."

"*Senor*, Cuban food is the best food in the world," the desk clerk bridled. "By this time all the paladars, the private cafes, are booked for the evening, but many *touristas* like our little warehouse – *La Bodeguita del Medio*. It is six blocks from here, in Empedrado Street."

"Gracias, senor. Eso es muy agradable de usted," Jane said, with measured courtesy. But even civility expressed in his native language could not allay the desk clerk's deep-seated hostility this time.

"De nada. A propósito - I would recommend the pork. They understand pig in that place. "

"Ow!" John stopped short, as if in great pain. He flailed and thrashed a moment, and seemed to be trying to reach around and grasp something sharp located just out of reach between his shoulder blades. Jane looked at him in alarm. He dropped his arms as suddenly as he had raised them and grinned back at the desk clerk. "No worries. Just trying to pull the knife out of my back."

Jane pursed her lips as they emerged onto the humid street, strangely mottled with the lengthening bluish shadows of a thousand paper doves. She pushed her sunglasses firmly up her nose, "I don't suppose I can even think of showing him who he's dealing with," she ventured in a wistful tone.

"No, no. Fair's fair. And he's just a little guy. Let him live."

"You're a much nicer person than I am," Jane sighed.

"But you're a much better shot," John said consolingly. "It all evens out."

5 HASTA SIEMPRE

It was the cocktail hour and the bar was a zoo, packed with people of many countries, all of them trying to Sharpie their assorted names and banalities onto the densely scribbled walls. Handed a pen, John reached up next to Salvador Allende's signature and wrote on a somewhat less enscrawled patch of blue: "Love! Love until the night collapses." "Cheerful," Jane tried to say, but her words were drowned out.

Seguiremos adelante

Como junto a tí seguimos

Y con Fidel te decimos
Hasta siempre Comandante

(We will carry on
As we followed you then
And with Fidel we say to you
Until always Commander)

The band inside had everyone singing a rousing version of *"Hasta Siempre,"* while the bands outside did not wait their turn in silence, but set up competing serenades designed to separate tourists from their hard currency sooner rather than later, on the theory that later was a mug's game. Everyone was impatient to get inside, where the musicians stood to make fifteen minutes worth of pesos and the tourists stood to get famously drunk; or at any rate to get drunk in a place famous people had been known to frequent.

21

To this end, the bar and its patrons seemed to have an understanding. Neither was interested in a long-term relationship; the tourists for the most part wanted to check off one more box on their vacation itinerary and move along, while the bar was happiest when its patrons drank, paid, and disappeared. So the queue progressed fairly quickly. The maitre d' seemed surprised when John requested a table, as if no sane human being would deliberately choose to sit and soak up the overwrought atmosphere for the length of time it would take to consume a meal.

"Hay un problema?" John asked, a little tired of the rote antagonism.

"Senor, it is just that you are not wearing the t-shirt." The maitre d' leaned forward to make himself heard. "Usually the ones who eat come wearing the Hemingway t-shirt. Or the Che. *Sigame, por favor."*

Easier said than done. The crowd was massed with particular intransigence around the old-fashioned wooden bar where a single bartender performed real magic, making twenty and thirty *mojitos* at a clip. It was quite a show. From a crate behind the bar, a pretty waitress pulled gleaming highball glasses, which she tossed one at a time to the *mojito* maestro, "Hey! Hey! Hey!" Having set his glasses in a precise row, the bartender started an assembly line, measuring out a tablespoon of sugar each, followed by a hit of fresh lime juice poured across the mouths of the glasses in a single pass, topped with a small tight wad of mint leaves, and enlivened with a spritz of soda. Hey! Hey! Hey! A quick muddle with a wooden pestle got each concoction foaming, at which point a generous measure of rum was added, again in a smooth unbroken sweep. Four ice cubes, a pink straw, and it was all over but the quaffing. Cheers and applause! The bartender took a bow.

Two entire *mojito* floorshows later, John and Jane finally managed to edge through the throng to claim a small battered table in a back room that opened onto a sliver of garden hung with Christmas lights and Chinese lanterns.

"I feel like I just summitted Annapurna," Jane said, half collapsing into her seat.

John sat down with his back to the door. "Would you call that a peak experience?"

"Careful. I'll start singing something from 'The Sound of Music.' 'The Lonely Goatherd' maybe?" Jane pretended to be studying the laminated menu in front of her.

"You know I love it when you yodel," John said, bending over his menu in turn. "And speaking of goat –"

"*Senor*, we are out of the goat tonight," the waiter said dolefully, setting down two *mojitos*.

"How's the snapper?" Jane wondered.

"*Senora*, we are out of the snapper tonight," the waiter desponded, wiping his hands on his backside.

"The curry?" John essayed, looking at Jane.

"*Senor*, we –"

"Tell you what," John held out the menus to the waiter, with a ten-dollar bill on top. "You order for us. All we ask is that you keep the *mojitos* coming."

The waiter hesitated. "It could be there is some goat remaining – an order or two."

"We're in your hands, *amigo*," John said, as though much depended on this. Jane leaned forward, smiling coyly. John leaned forward, in comic imitation. The waiter's hand, holding a dual flame zippo lighter, intruded between them.

"*Perdoname.*" He had returned to light the votive candle in its knobbly little fishbowl. He only burned himself twice in the attempt.

"You were saying?" John prodded, when they were alone again.

Jane indicated the garden with her chin. "Strings of lights. Paper lanterns. Takes me back."

"Colombia," John recalled, catching her drift. "One step ahead of the *Autodefensas*. That flower looked good in your hair." They clinked glasses and drank.

The *mojitos* were on the weak side, but good and cold. The music drifted in, the closest diners in the nearest rooms drifted out. The votive candle and a beat up chandelier overhead created a soft shell of light around them. For a moment life was good. Into that moment came a vigorously ancient and ostentatiously blind fortune-teller, chewing a huge unlit cigar and dressed in speckless white like a Western bride. Or an Asian corpse. A small, well-scrubbed boy with a carney's cheek and a con man's flair for patter guided her to the table.

"Hey lady! My *abuela* wants to tell your fortune."

Jane smiled faintly. "I already met a tall handsome stranger."

The fortune-teller pulled the *Presidente* out of her mouth and stuck it in her lacy white turban. "This is a message, not a divination, *senora*. The Orishas wish to speak."

"Two for the price of one," the boy parleyed. He held out his hand and, after exchanging a skeptical but resigned glance with Jane, John slipped the kid a fiver.

"Who are the Orishas?" Jane leaned forward to ask the child.

He replied by putting a finger to his lips. "Shhhh!" His grandmother was silent a moment, then began to hum and sway. The humming gave way to a garbled sort of chant that distilled into an ominous drone of words.

"Your future is both dark and dangerous," she intoned.

"Classic!" John gave Jane a thumbs-up.

The little boy frowned heavily and shook his head at John, who obediently wilted into silence, to Jane's amusement.

The fortune-teller was deep into her act. "I see —" she paused and shuddered theatrically. Dropped her voice to a hushed whisper. "Monsters." The chanting resumed, presumably to build suspense and allow her point to sink in. "But," she burst out and froze. Again with the melodrama. Jane closed one eye in irritation. "The Orishas ask that you remember. Who. You. Are," the old woman admonished, stabbing a fat and paste-bejeweled finger at John for emphasis.

"I give up. Who are we?" Jane asked, her eyes straying to the turban and the fat black cigar, which had begun to smolder slightly. The merest wisp of a curl of smoke rose like incense toward the ceiling.

"The Orishas want to remind you that you are Chango and Oshun, the gods of war and beauty on earth." Lifting her arms and her sightless eyes heavenward, the fortune teller paused as though lost in thought, then dropped her arms and head abruptly. Jane and John looked politely unconvinced.

"Just so you know," Jane clarified for John, "I'm war and you're beauty."

"That it?" John inquired, trying to keep the edge of impatience out of his voice.

Her chin tucked almost into her broad bosom, the fortune-teller answered in a guttural voice that seemed to come from a world beyond. "You are also to remember that there is such a thing as right *ashe*." John and Jane looked at her with renewed interest and respect. In the Exorcist, that kind of vocal effect required computers and a voiceover. She raised her head and looked at them with burning milk-white eyes. "What others call *karma*."

The waiter arrived with fresh drinks and in the farther room – by coincidence? - a new band was striking up the dance of *Oshun y Chango*. A troupe of dancers in elaborate gold and red costumes pulled tourists from their inert cliques and bar stools and made them join in. The fortune-teller's grandson tugged at Jane's hand.

Closing her eyes again, the fortune-teller gestured toward the far room. "Go, child. What you don't understand, you learn in the dance." Jane threw John a look of mischievous surrender and let the child lead her. John watched as she found a place in the circle of dancers, and almost immediately caught the rhythm and the moves, earning the instantaneous and very audible admiration of the predominantly male spectators.

"Drink?" turning back to the table, John held out one of the as yet untouched mojitos, which the fortune-teller graciously and unerringly accepted. Without opening her unseeing eyes.

"The Orishas are pleased," she declared.

John lifted his glass politely. "If they're happy, I'm happy."

She drained her glass the way Tiger Woods plays golf; that is, with singular grace and smooth efficiency. Her flawless technique would have put most frat pledges to shame. John was so lost in admiration that he jumped slightly when she set the glass back on the table with a snap. "You do not understand. Everything is wrong. And everything now depends on you. The two of you. THAT," she said sardonically, "Is IT." Her grandson reappeared as she turned to go, and they left by way of the back door, picking their way through the rear garden with its ragged constellation of tables, potted plants, and flagstones. In the far room, the dance was reaching some sort of crescendo, full of wild drumming and banshee shrieks. By sitting sideways in his chair, John could see Jane hiking up her skirt, kicking off her shoes, and matching the lead dancer move for move. Just when it seemed the music could not get any louder and the dancers could not whirl and thrust any faster, there was a blinding flash. Every light in the place flared on at once. Followed by total darkness as every light went out – even the fairy lights in the garden, even the votive candle on the table, snuffed out by an errant gust of wind. Amid screams and shouts in many languages, John sat tight. A shadow slid across his line of vision as the lights in the bar flickered on again, then off again to nervous laughter. The trumpeter blew a false note or two as the band tried to pick up where they had left off.

John palmed a fork from the table as a cold metal chain whipped across his throat.

6 CLOSING TIME

The light fixture overhead did not leap back to life. But in the wan light eking in from the bar, John saw that a small man occupied Jane's seat. A very small man, a biker dude in miniature, who seemed utterly focused on lighting a small cigar. The wooden match he cradled in one hand illuminated his face like a Rembrandt self-portrait, albeit a very hirsute and vividly colored Rembrandt self-portrait; for every square centimeter of skin bore either the dye injected by a tattoo needle or an overgrowth of facial hair. Willy Nelson would have envied his pony-tail. He wore wraparound Eye Ride sunglasses, which he did not remove, and which may have contributed to the difficulty he had getting his stogie evenly lit. For what seemed an eternity he rolled it gently this way and that, patiently puffing away with the most intense concentration. When at last he had the smoke drawing smoothly, he extinguished the match and tossed it over his shoulder onto the floor. With the weird insouciance of the psychotic, he patted each of his pockets in turn until he remembered he had left the matchbox on the table. Whistling tunelessly through gold teeth, he extracted and lit another match, reignited the votive candle, extinguished the second match, and sent it to join its brother on the floor. Still whistling, he replaced the matchbox in an inner pocket and paused as though in thought. When he withdrew his hand again, he was holding a Glock 30, which he proceeded to fire into the air. Just a round or two. No biggie.

Apparently everybody in the bar, Cubans and tourists alike, spoke Glock, because in a New York minute the place cleared out. The throng inside and the throng outside collided briefly, then re-oriented and ran away together as fast as their individual legs and health status would

27

permit, melting to nothing like so many ice floes in a warming Arctic sea. Two intrepid souls remained behind in the bar: one of the busboys, an enterprising youngster who crouched on the floor near the old-fashioned cash register, presumably daring life and limb to clean out the cash drawer, and Jane, who leaned against a door jamb, clutching her stiletto-heeled Manolo Blahniks to her chest and straining to hear what was said.

The small biker dude addressed his junior partner, who had practically drawn John out of his seat, so tight was the heavy-duty chain around his neck.

"Fils de pute, 'Fifi. Tu me fais chier. I said 'kill the lights,' not the waiter." ("Son of a bitch, 'Fifi. You're pissing me off here.") From this exchange a portion of John's brain deduced that the small biker dude might be French Canadian. Oh shit, his brain further deduced.

The younger biker, whose full name was Rififi and who might best be described as a cross between a homicidal Wookie and a downy baby chick, turned red and tried to explain. "Pardon, Bob. His head got in the way."

Bob rolled his eyes and you got the feeling such minor mishaps were an all too frequent source of irritation. *"C'est rien que del la merde. Tête de noeud.* You can't just go around killing people in a foreign country. Do you even know who to bribe here? No." ("That's bullshit. What a dickhead.")

"Pardon, Bob. I thought *you* must know. Because we will be killing this one, *n'est ce pas?"*

"How many times must I repeat, there is killing and there is killing." He divided the world using both hands. "Civilians and –"

Meanwhile John was quietly choking but trying to interrupt, one hand grasping the chain to prevent total strangulation, the other raised in polite one-fingered query: *"Excusez-moi?"*

Both men paused in their discussion and looked blankly at their detainee, whose fate had momentarily been subordinated to a review of best criminal practices. Bob's face cleared. He tapped his forehead with the sleek snub-nosed barrel of his gun and playfully wagged the gun back at John. "One dickhead leads to another. You remind me that time is money and we are short on both. *Bon!* Let us begin again. Monsieur Doe. *Bon soir! Enchante!* It has been some time since last we met. But no doubt you remember Quebec?"

"Could you be a little more specif-" John gurgled and tore at the chain as Rififi conscientiously tightened it.

"The Mounties wore red, you wore leather? Undercover *pauvre con* (asshole)." He watched to see whether or not memory was dawning for John. It was. It had. A small matter of half a dozen gangs and several dozen corpses.

"Eh? *Mais oui!* So now you know who is snuffing you out like a candle." He extinguished the votive candle between his thumb and forefinger. It may have hurt. There was a slight hissing sound. *"Voila!"*

"You know, some people might say you owed me." Rififi leaned down to see whether John was serious. "After all, I cleared out your competition. More for you."

"Oui, mon frère. We owe you," Bob guffawed. "20% of net for the past three years. More for you – or rather more for those you used to represent. A 20% tax remitted monthly to a PO box in Nevada. So you can appreciate how I have looked forward to finding you and settling old scores. Also it doesn't hurt that there is a bounty to be claimed. Only 50 thousand to be sure, but in this economy-" he shrugged in true Gallic fashion.

John stopped struggling altogether. "Wait – what?"

"I know. A pittance, right? Why bother? With us it's a case of serendipity, pure and simple. We were here on totally unrelated business –"

"Une affaire de prostituée," Rififi explained.

Bob paused, glared until his sidekick wilted, then resumed: "- which turned out to be a trifle premature. But just as we decide the trip is a bust – we spot you in the square. And just like that," he snaps his fingers,

"We cover our expenses, we get brownie points with the big boys, we maybe make a profit on your lady friend –"

"The ebay," Rififi used one hand to show John the picture he had taken of Jane with his cell phone, punching a button to display a string of bids submitted by clients eager to buy.

"So you see? It's all good! As the spoiled children of your narcissistic country say. 'Fifi!" Bob made a slashing gesture across his own throat with the barrel of his gun.

"Why, darling," Jane said, appearing in the doorway, still barefoot and twirling her shoes like six-guns. "I was beginning to think you had forgotten." She shifted the shoes to one hand and held out the other to Bob. "It's my birthday and he promised me an orgy. You must be – "

"Bob," Rififi prompted, when Bob was slow to respond.

"Bouffon," Bob spat at his sidekick. But he shifted his cigar to his mouth and his gun to his left hand and got up to greet Jane. Like a moth to the blowtorch.

"Bob," he repeated.

"Bob." She took his right hand caressingly, alluringly in her own. "And I," she crooned, leaning in seductively as though intending to exchange a cheek kiss, French fashion, "am Lady Lazarus."

They had no idea what hit them, poor lambs. In a swift blur of motion, Jane backhanded Rififi with her shoes, twisted Bob's arm behind him and laid him out on the concrete floor, where an elbow to the skull knocked him out cold. Stunned as much by Jane's performance as the blow she had dealt him, Rififi seemed hardly to feel the purloined fork when John drove it into his thigh. John twisted free with relative ease and just as Rififi appeared to awaken to his change of fortune, John hoist him with his own petard, which is to say John confiscated Rififi's own heavy duty chain and slammed him upside the head with it. The ungentle giant crumbled to the ground like a tall building wired for demolition. Jane neatly stood aside, tucking the Glock in her purse.

John looked at Jane. "I take back everything I said about those shoes."

"When I think of the shit you gave me!" Jane said, steadying herself against him as she slipped them back on. "It always pays to buy the best. But it's true what they say about being unemployed and losing your skills. That was a little sloppy."

"Beg to differ. But we were lucky on the moron scale. Ten more IQ points," John glanced at the prostrate bikers, "And it could have been ugly."

As they prepared to leave, several policemen and a Sidney Greenstreet look-alike in a white suit and Panama hat entered the bar, followed at a timorous distance by the rest of the restaurant staff. The policemen hastened to tend to Bob and company. Sid stopped before John and Jane and doffed his *ultrafino* chapeau.

"I am an influential and respected man," John muttered to Jane.

"You'd look good in a hat," Jane opined in a whisper.

"On behalf of the Cuban Tourist Board, I most humbly apologize for any unpleasantness," Sid said, bowing. A whiff of bay rum diffused toward them, pleasantly spicy.

"Ordinarily such things require a call to the relevant embassy." The expressions on John's and Jane's faces grew brittle at the thought. "We express contrition, they express concern. Additional pleasantries and assurances are exchanged. Alas," Sid sighed, "our respective countries have no formal relations at present, so I am afraid the pleasantries stop here." John and Jane sagged slightly in relief and tried to mirror Sid's regret. "We've had our eye on these two," Sid continued, indicating Rififi and Bob as they were bundled past. "Canadians, but they have the American disease. Here we say 'It's in the water.'" He held out a fancy wooden box of Cohiba cigars, a bottle of Havana Club, and a small gift bag. Then he bowed again, this time indicating the door. "Don't drink the water, senor, senora. If you know what's good for you."

Strolling back to their room through Old Havana's romantic squares and exotic byways, John whipped out his Blackberry and started doing currency conversions.

"Oh look," Jane said, reaching into the gift bag and pulling out a Che

Guevara t-shirt.

"Fifty thousand?! Did you hear that? Three months ago it was almost half a million. Each. And the Canadian dollar is way down; which makes it – whoa. $45,000."

"Hmmm," Jane considered, examining the bottle of Havana Club. "About 12,000 Happy Meals. Or one Louis Vuitton handbag."

7 SMOKE GETS IN YOUR EYES

Under the ruthless glare of too many fluorescent lights, the walls of the Western Union lobby were screamingly yellow for that hour of the morning. Lines of Cubans waiting to collect remittances sent by relatives in the U.S., Spain, and elsewhere snaked from every teller's window. Cheery Latin muzak kept the lines moving with fair efficiency. From behind dark glasses and with their luggage beside them, John and Jane stood at a sunny yellow check desk nursing petite paper cups of café con leche and a couple of economy-sized hangovers as they slogged through an absurd amount of paperwork. It did not help that every available pen was either out of ink or short enough to run dry after a stroke or two.

"OK, I've gotten to the part about signing over our first born child," John quipped.

"Yeah. They were asking about my immortal soul a minute ago," Jane said. "Under intangible collateral. Here." They traded stacks of paper and continued signing in silence. John finished first. He gazed at Jane so intently that she paused and looked back at him, eyebrows raised.

"Yes?"

"I say we make a few calls. You have to figure the heat is off. Under $50K American. That's not just uncool – that's downright cold. I had 18 years in, you had –"

"Same," Jane insisted. When he looked skeptical she said, "They got me fresh out of prep school. Yale? Hello."

"Yeah, but the point is, I'm offended. $50K offends me. Aren't you offended? Jeez."

"Bargain basement," Jane agreed.

"Which brings up that whole Macy's-Gimbel's thing. Your outfit versus mine. Didn't Macy's buy Gimbel's?"

Jane looked at him over her sunglasses. "I shop Barney's"

"All I'm saying is – we don't really know what happened. Who bought who, which merged with what, or why we went from assets to liabilities like that," John snapped his fingers.

"Downsizing is a bitch. Welcome to the decline of the middle class," Jane shrugged.

"What – that was a reduction in force? We got RIFed?" John snorted, thinking of all the HR policies that would have to be rewritten. "OK, how do you explain the bounty then? It's like a fraction of what it was, 10 percent. Just two months ago."

"After-Christmas sale? Now for a limited time only... C'mon. What's the common thread here? They're cheap bastards. If they dropped the price it's because they can. Supply and demand. Econ 101."

"Or maybe," John countered, "maybe what we have here is somebody protecting their backside, and not all that convincingly. Somebody made a mistake. And yes they're holding onto this fig leaf. But they're sending a signal."

"A notice in the Times would have done," Jane observed drily.

"What's wrong with putting out a few feelers? What's wrong," John spoke quickly, knowing it was a leap but wanting to get it out there, "with asking for our jobs back?"

Jane looked at him steadily. A young woman with a stroller and sleeping infant stopped close by, reached in between them to rifle through the forms, failed to find what she was looking for, moved on. Finally Jane said, "Why don't we just apply for unemployment and tell them where to send the check?"

"No, come on, think about it. Years of training, all our experience, not to mention all the shit we know – like I said, we're assets, human capital. Why should they want to destroy the investment we represent?"

"You mean aside from all the shit we know, not to mention all the shit we've done?" Jane said. "You tell me. I have no idea why being accidentally married to a competing spook is a firing offense, much less a capital crime."

"Bingo," John said.

"What?"

"'Accidentally married.' Who would believe neither of us knew?"

"They were in merger talks. We were already merged. That should have been a plus."

"Two for the price of one," John nodded.

"Thank you, Mr. Walmart. But that is my point. Why kill off your future? I'm thinking if we do anything we should start by appealing to a higher power." They were standing in the shortest line, the one for foreign nationals, when she said this.

"I've heard God and Caesar have an understanding, something about separate checks, going dutch?" John pretended to be searching his memory.

"I've been thinking we should take this to Uncle Charlie." The Italian gentleman in front of them who had been trading Euros finished his currency exchange and gave a double-take as he turned to leave and Jane caught his eye. He passed by slowly, lingering over his money, his wallet, and Jane. John cocked his head, putting his arm around Jane and baring his teeth in an annoyed smile.

"Ballsy," he commented, watching the Italian leave the bank. At the revolving door, the man kissed his fingers in Jane's direction and John waved. "You know that guy?"

"I have one of those faces. And I was a Glock Girl?" Jane said, handing the sheaf of papers to the cashier. "No hair-trigger puns, please."

"I'm too mesmerized by the image of you hawking mass market tupperware. But back to Uncle Charlie. It is ballsy. But bright?"

"*You* sound like you're planning to ask them over for cucumber sandwiches or something. Kind of hard to keep a porch light on when you don't have a porch." The cashier carefully counted out the money. Once. Twice. It wasn't all that much, compared to the old days, but it was a fortune in that place, not to mention the end of their marital nest egg. Jane handed John half the stack of bills, pretending not to feel the stony, incredulous stares of the Cubans who were there to receive $10, $20, $50 in hard currency. Like a well-rehearsed vaudeville act, John and Jane tucked the remains of their worldly wealth into their inner jacket pockets, adjusted their sunglasses, and reached for their pullmans.

8 MY OLD SCHOOL

Outside the Western Union, a flurry of Cubans complicated the sidewalk. A dump truck spewed diesel fumes and soot. Tiny round coco taxis in tropical fruit colors sputtered past in search of early sightseers. John waved them off. A block onward the people and the traffic thinned, the crumbling beauty of old Havana came to an abrupt halt, and the five-mile expanse of waterfront known as the Malecon opened out before them beneath a cloudy, troubled sky.

The buildings lining this section of the Malecon were in dire straits and for the most part empty. Despite the million dollar views, UNESCO heritage site restoration funds had dried up in the global economic downturn. Last year's hurricane had left the tenements and storefronts looking like the densely scaffolded and disintegrating ruins of a lost civilization. For now, their singular saving grace was that they kept the relentless winds and corrosive salt-spray from too perniciously visiting the rest of the city. But the panorama they presented was disquieting. Or so it seemed to Jane and John, who took their conversation across the broad boulevard to the curving seawall that provided an expansive vista of the city in all its glory and decay. The wall was low enough to sit on. The tide was out. The waves kept their distance. Far down the esplanade, a few dispirited dogs were walking their dispirited people. Almost directly below the spot John and Jane chose to park themselves, Ernest Hemingway's old man was setting out in a small dinghy for another play date with an ill-tempered sea. Seagulls dipped and dove above an ancient dumpster. A sense of collapse and doomed endings briefly overwhelmed speech.

"Who do you suppose came up with that color scheme?" Jane said at last, indicating a grouping of facades picked out in gaudy yellows, greens, and pinks.

"Pope soap," John said. "John Paul was here - ten years ago? Yeah. They spruced the place up." Jane swiveled to look at him. "Now it can be told. You're married to an altar boy. 'Agnus Dei, qui tolis peccata mundi, miserere nobis.'" He made the sign of the cross in her general direction. "My family made wine for the nuns."

"That would explain the goody-two-shoes streak," Jane said.

"And my appreciation of strong drink." John shook his head slightly at a young prostitute who was dawdling in front of them, and got down to brass tacks. "I think it's better if we start by talking to Vinnie."

Jane watched the prostitute switch directions and sway off in pursuit of a slow-moving bicycle. She crossed her legs and examined the cracking pavement under her feet a moment before transferring her attention back to John. "So - call Vinnie and come with me to Davos," she opened the bargaining flirtatiously.

John countered by taking her hand and holding it open against his own so that their wedding rings touched. "So call Uncle Charlie and come with me to Brooklyn."

"Not the same. Charlie and I – don't have that kind of relationship. That's funny?" she tried to snatch her hand back.

"That's kind of like saying you and Santa Claus don't have that kind of a relationship. Charlie is a legend and an institution. I've never even seen the guy. For all I know Charlie is a myth."

"You don't retire a myth. Charlie's wife died last spring – "

"He was married?"

"Car crash."

"Ah."

"Yeah," Jane said, affirming that she was thinking what he was thinking. In some lines of work there are no accidents. "He retired in December."

"And we know this because…"

She shrugged. "I keep up. Bloomberg. The Times. Despite everything, they threw him a big White House shindig. What do you do when you're online anyway?"

"Poker? Blackjack? Danger Room?" he gave her hand a playful tug. She wasn't feeling playful.

"He lives in Davos. And it's January. They all go to Davos in January, so it won't be hard to blend in."

"They who?"

"Oh you know - all of them. The bigwigs. Everybody who's anybody. It's that annual circle jerk for the rich and shameless. The what-is-it." She snapped her fingers repeatedly, searching for the exact term. "World Economic Forum?" When he didn't answer immediately, she put her chin up. "Breaking team so soon? That didn't take long."

Still holding her hand, John turned and squinted out to sea in the direction of the marina and the boat. "Hold on. Same team. Same mission. Different trajectories - to get this resolved. Maybe." The ocean breeze stiffened, pushing a lock of Jane's long hair across her face. John caressingly tucked it behind her ear. "Do you even know - ?"

Jane slid down off the seawall and faced John. "I know Vinnie can't get us our jobs back. I know Vinnie is a nobody. There is no way he can crack a joke and restore the miracle of the paycheck. Much less wipe us off the kill list."

In his friend's defense, but also because directly accosting a big gun, one of the biggest, seemed a bit rash, John said pointedly, "It's the somebodies who are out to get us."

Jane drew a deep breath and stepped backward, her mind made up. "Where I'm going you can't follow – "

The pain and concern showed in John's face, but he knew his lines and he spoke them without hesitation: "What I've got to do, you can't be any part of." He had to raise his voice on the last few words. She was already walking away, trailing her black pullman. "You're going to trust me with the boat?"

She stopped short. "I'd say 'keep the home fires burning,' but you might take that the wrong way."

John gave it one last shot. "You're on a wild goose chase. Do they even have an airport in this country?"

"Big on birds?" Jane flung back, jokingly, waving with her full hand and then giving him the finger. "Read between the lines."

John grinned. "Didn't mean to ruffle your feathers," he called.

Jane laughed mockingly, her reply just barely drifting back to him, "Tweet me!"

9 SLOOP JOHN B

"You mean to say she trusted you with the boat?"

"I know, right?" John flashed a wan smile. "It's her baby. But if it's got an engine, I can drive it. The hardest part was getting out of the harbor." As he spoke, everything pitched slightly, including John himself. But the squall had mostly blown itself out; the great grey elephant swells had diminished to choppy whitecaps and the worst was past. Outside the portholes a metallic disk of sun rolled westward through an endless succession of second-rate clouds. It was just four o'clock. The espresso pot could be heard percolating on the tiny stove in the galley.

"Well, you've managed to catch me at my tea, which is rather bad form," Gerald complained. And there he sat, with his china teacup, a pair of silver tongs poised to select a wafer thin slice of lemon. "I'm a union shop, you know. Time and a half outside of normal hours."

"A working class hero is something to be. No rest for the unemployed, though. I'm trying to show a little initiative here. Surprise the little woman."

"Excellent notion, old chap, you are to be commended. I've done grousing. Where is our lovely lass, by the by? Have you had her surgically removed? I think it was Wilde who said 'The most dangerous food a man can eat is wedding cake.'" Gerald mused, reaching for a McVities Rich Tea biscuit.

41

"True enough, if Jane baked it. But to cut to the chase, at one point we had discussed applying for a small business loan - " John began.

"Maintaining radio silence, I'm with you. Hush-hush on the Jane front. Mum's the word. As for your small business start-up - hmmm. Even if the taps of capitalism were flowing – which they are not – it would be a little sticky, coming from here. That whole offshore tax haven thing. But definitely do-able, give or take a double-reverse merger or two. You're a veteran? That helps. Care to identify the line of business? I should mention that anything to do with import/export almost always gets the go-ahead."

"Security services?" John hazarded.

"More like insecurity services, if I understand you. But I believe it is a growth industry, given current trends. I would just mention, taking the long view you know, that winner-take-all vastly increases the stakes and probabilities for all the losers? If one happened to be a betting man."

"Unless the game is rigged."

"I can see you have given this some little thought. Alrighty then – will do." He took a sip of tea. "Ah. That adds heart to a man. Before I go, did you want me to contact Sotheby's about the Cezanne?"

John thought a minute. "No. No, not just yet. But if anything happens to me -"

"Say no more. We've agreed to keep Jane out of the kitchen, which is half the battle. Ta, then," Gerald reached a hand forward to Skype out.

"Ta," John echoed. The espresso pot gurgled a warning. In the galley, he automatically got down two cups. Sighed. Put one back.

10 STAY VISIBLE

The lobby of the Hotel Schatzalp was surprisingly cheery for a former TB sanatorium and Nazi hangout. Entering through intricately carved Art Nouveau doors from a landscape of dazzling white, you were met (once your eyes adjusted) by the interior design equivalent of sweetness and light. Buttercup-tinted walls, stained glass windows blooming with lilies and vines, a herd of overstuffed ivory-covered furniture grazing on Persian carpets in the palest shades of leaf, sunshine, and cream. Only the great checkerboard of the black and white marble flooring hinted at a more conflicted reality.

The concierge in his gilded cage was multi-lingual and beautiful in that melting, Rudolph Valentino, Sheik of Araby sort of way. Recognizing in Jane a bird of his feather, he smiled and inclined his head in welcome.

"Je recherché Monsieur Charles Acton," Jane murmured in a low and intimate tone, looking at the concierge over her sunglasses. ("I'm looking for Mr. Charles Acton.")

"Vous avez un rendez-vous?" In European fashion, the concierge allowed his gaze to travel appreciatively over all of Jane that he could see without leaving his post or boorishly craning. ("You have an appointment?")

"Non," Jane shook her head and allowed her brow to cloud. *"Mais il est primordial."* ("No. But it is of the utmost importance.")

His face reflecting her concern, the concierge explained that the gentleman had gone for a walk down toward the village and could be found in or around the local cemetery. This was a daily ritual, and not all that unusual. After all, his wife was buried there, along with the painter Kirchner and an unknown number of anonymous Jews murdered at Buchenwald.

"Vous l'apprecierez!" he assured her. *"Il est tres célèbre, tres historique. Un emplacement de patrimoine mondial."* ("You will enjoy it! It is very famous, very historical.")

"A cemetery." What's more, a cemetery with a wife in it. Jane thanked the concierge and thought fleetingly of John, who without knowing anything had somehow known better. Advancing from square to square on her way out, Jane muttered, "Yeah, that figures."

11 WE BOTH GO DOWN TOGETHER

It was a long cold walk back down the road toward town, the dry snow crunching under foot. The glories of the Swiss scenery registered briefly, but Jane hit a slick patch and prudently redirected her attention to more immediate concerns – 1) any hint of movement in the frozen landscape and 2) not breaking her own fool neck. At the Zurich airport she had traded her heels for boots at the Burberry duty-free shop and snagged a no-nonsense gray wool topcoat at Hugo Boss; but the alpen air was briskly implacable and the temperature was dipping even further as the sun dropped like a frigid white stone toward the westward mountains. At the signpost, she took the narrow and mostly unbroken left hand track, plunging straightway into the forest. The ominous strains of "Finlandia" seemed to grow louder with every labored step.

Around the first bend, the cemetery began with a waist-high stone fence. Looking over the fence, among the many trees Jane glimpsed a roughhewn marker here, an odd wooden cross with a peaked roof there. A few raw cleared spaces in the thickets and the undergrowth. Those burial sites were an advance guard of sorts, settlers and unwelcome intruders in the kingdom of trees. Further on, the trees thinned out and the graves multiplied. Here the comparatively ancient deceased lay buried, the original colony, close to the ruins of a fifteenth century kirche. And over them stood the original trees, sparse in number, but towering higher than the eye could comfortably follow and holding their ground like stern primeval gods. Just in front of the arched entry into the cemetery, a tall dark figure stood hunched against the wind, gazing across the vista of cracked and moldering headstones.

The figure turned only its craggy head in Jane's direction as she approached. A sharp gust raked at the brush of white hair a younger man would not have bothered with, but otherwise the man in his black muffler and overcoat remained as motionless as one of the obelisks in the graveyard before him. Neither Jane nor the man spoke until they were within perhaps two feet of one another. Then the man resumed his surveillance of the dead and said: "I don't know you and I can't help you."

"But you know it's all some colossal misunderstanding."

"I know nothing of the sort."

"You knew ten years ago," she said evenly. He let the wind answer for him. She tried again. "If we could just talk to somebody. We always – both of us, separately, together, right down the line – played it by the book. We always did exactly what we were supposed to do."

"With one slight exception," he said with icy, heart-stopping deliberation, squinting at something only he could see.

"Which could be said to prove the rule," Jane countered, at the same time stunned by his total lack of irony. "Even there, the most extreme case imaginable, we - did the right thing. We did not follow an unlawful order. No court would expect someone either to kill their spouse or to accept execution without a trial."

"Leaving aside that the appeal to law is laughable, you do realize you wiped out an entire graduating class?"

"You do realize the decision to make us a final exam was arrived at without our input, much less our consent? No judgment!" she held up one hand as he looked at her and looked away again. "But they're penalizing the wrong parties. Not that we want to blow the whistle. We're team players, always have been. We just want things back the way they were."

"Young woman," he began.

"'Young woman?'" she echoed derisively. "That's rich, Charles."

He continued speaking as if she had not spoken. "A short time ago your business associates tried to kill you. Read something into that. The ground has shifted. The game has changed. There is no job, there is no security. That world is gone." He turned his back and walked away from her a few steps before stopping to cast one last comment over his shoulder. "For me too, by the way. So you see, you really are on your own, cookie. We're all on our own." The last line was uttered almost under his breath.

"Could you at least tell me why?" she asked, and the last word hung in the air like something strung between them.

In answer, he thrust his hands deeper into his pockets, hunched forward against the cold, and trudged away from her toward the deeper woods.

12 CALAMITY SONG

Once more crunching down the road toward Davos, Jane thought about calling John.   That was one call she did not want to make. "Honey, we hit a dead end in a Swiss cemetery."   Total fail.   And score one for John.   Turned out her ace in the hole was nothing but a bonehead move.   Alrighty then.   This much was certain: she and John were officially outside.   Out in the cold.   Both in spy parlance and, in her case, literally.   She shivered with grim amusement.   They had no idea why, it made no sense, but there it was.   End of story.

And now she had a train to catch.   Beyond that, the future loomed a little darker and a little more dangerous than before.   Fortunately she was pressed for time, so she allowed herself the luxury of taking the Scarlet O'Hara approach.   She would think about it tomorrow.

As she entered Davos proper, the snowy hummocks of the less-travelled Obere Strasse thinned to a polite veneer of ice about five feet before the Promenade began.   Already the streetlights shone muddily over a crepuscular swarm of uber-wealthy transnationals, the global elites who turned sleepy Davos into a sort of glitzy Epcot Center every January.   An empty horse-drawn sleigh trotted into view, harness bells jangling with forced merriment along the flanks of a world-weary appaloosa.   Jane tussled with her need to speed to catch the Zurich train and a reluctance to burden the horse, whose downcast demeanor shrieked forced labor and in whose eyes she read a glint of suppressed mutiny.   "Fuck it," she murmured and was about to plunge into the crowd on shank's mare when two mildly intoxicated, innately loutish hedge fund types accosted her.   Visually indistinguishable except for their "Hi, I'm

Bernie"-"Hi, I'm Howie" WEF nametags (embellished with the blue dot of million dollar donorship), they presented as stereotypes of Wall Street entitlement gone wild, decked out in designer everything and screamingly over-accessorized by a couple of leather-bound bodyguards.

"Oh! Oh! There she is. That's her," Howie piped up, first pointing at Jane, then grabbing her upper arm. Jane tensed to respond with an elbow-strike to his windpipe, when she saw that Bernie was backing off and looking doubtful.

"I dunno, man. She looks a little-" he spread his fingers and waggled his hand, palm down, the international sign for 'iffy.'

Howie stepped back, both hands outstretched toward Jane, shoulders hunched in disbelief. "You crazy asshole. Bernard. You got Venus on the fucking half-shell here..."

"Venus on the fucking half-shell was a fucking blonde," Bernie pointed out, feeling for a pack of smokes.

"Don't listen to him," Howie implored, "he's a crazy fucking asshole. He robs widows and orphans and charges them 20% for the privilege."

"Said the guy who's this close-" Bernie measured the air with forefinger and thumb, "to a federal indictment..."

Jane smiled icily and pivoted away. "I'm late for a train." This time it was Bernie who stepped forward to physically detain her.

"Oh whoa!" he said around his cigarette. "Listen to Miss Pay-Per-View here. Fuckin' A you're late – strike one. You're a dish, but come on. You're almost as old as my wife – strike two. And you are not a blonde – strike three."

Jane stared at his hand until he felt compelled to remove it. Then she said, thoughtfully, "You ordered a blonde, did you?"

"You've heard of bond ratings? We're into blonde ratings. And hyperinflation," Howie quipped, ogling after two extremely busty young women.

"And naked options," Jane riposted, her eyes narrowing. "No doubt."

Bernie rolled his eyes. "Asswit and company?" He wheeled in front of Howie and Jane to command their undivided attention. "Time is money. That is the be-all and end-all, the song of songs, the bottom line. Let's fill or kill here. You," he pointed at Jane with his cigarette, "are not the girl from the website; but if you're the package we were expecting, sugar, so be it." He walked around her as if she was a luxury car in a showroom. "And if you don't make the grade," he shrugged, "you go home tomorrow, COD."

Jane looked at Howie. She looked at Bernie. She reflected that she was running low on cash. Also that the two Wall Street assholes facing her belonged to the tribe that had trashed her pension fund. Without skipping a beat, she put an arm around each of them and lowered her voice conspiratorially. "Gentlemen, I think I understand the situation perfectly. You had a certain expectation and you're feeling a little exposed here. You look to me like the kind of guys who like to hedge your bets and limit your risk. So I'll tell you what I'm going to do. How about I put a little skin in the game?" And she nodded toward the Victoria's Secret shop across the street, where nubile and faceless manikins in push-up bras and thongs cavorted behind luridly backlit plate glass windows.

13 HOW TO BE A MILLIONAIRE

Like dancers in a music video, the five of them crossed the street in lock step to the lingerie shop. Howie held the door and Bernie snapped his fingers at the bodyguards. "Stay," he ordered and the two men stationed themselves on either side of the entrance, exuding testosterone and embarrassment. Once inside, a bevy of saleswomen in sleek black ensembles and perfect hair bore down upon them like so many Hollywood vampires. They relieved Howie and Bernie of their coats and conducted a whirlwind tour of the shop, reaping a vast collection of lacy nothings at Jane's unerring direction. When every leather, feather, sequined, and see-through fetish and fantasy was provided for, the saleswomen led the way upstairs to a private waiting room, a copy of Versailles's Hall of Mirrors in miniature, where Howie and Bernie were ensconced in comfortable club chairs, a decent bottle of scotch at their elbows.

"Does this come in - black?" Jane asked, flaunting a white fur-trimmed bustier and flashing her prospective sugar daddies an alluring smile. Immediately the saleswomen scurried below, and Jane turned to enter the changing room. "I'll be back before you can say 'credit default swap,'" she promised.

On the other side of the door, Jane studied the bustier the way a vegan contemplates a bloody veal chop, before tossing it over one shoulder and assessing her prospects of escape. It was a spacious gilt-trimmed chamber with the usual dais and three-sided mirror for preening. A series of velvet curtains concealed one, two, three alcoves where clients could disrobe in private and, behind curtain number four – a shallow stockroom, lined floor to ceiling with shelving and plastic bins, except for the far end where Swiss law provided a second floor emergency exit. Praying no fire alarms would go off, Jane darted to the heavy metal door and put her shoulder against it just as a discreet knock sounded from the waiting room and two pert saleswomen entered.

"Does madame require –" they stopped, stock still, mid-sentence, seeing their record-breaking commission poised to abscond. Jane clasped her hands in fear and supplication, then motioned them to her side.

"Sex traffickers. " she whispered urgently. "They've got three other girls drugged up and locked in a closet back at the hotel. If you'll call the police, I can sneak out and –"

They looked at each other, looked at her. Bewildered "But in this country, sex is - legal."

"And that is very enlightened of you," Jane conceded, "but they've taken our passports and threatened to kill us."

"Oh," one of the women gasped, putting her hands to her mouth. "I saw the men outside."

"We're headed for the worst little whorehouse in Abu Dhabi. Including my baby sister."

Another, louder knock fell on the door. "Hey, Blondie. If Daddy doesn't get a lap-dance pretty fucking soon, he's going to downgrade you to a sell."

Jane indicated the door with an open palm. "See?"

The saleswomen looked at each other, looked at Jane. Came down firmly on the side of sisterhood and solidarity. Almost in the same breath they recited the musketeer maxim. Which is also the national motto of Switzerland. *"Einer für alle, alle für einen.* Go!" They practically pushed her out the door.

It was a command that did not have to be repeated. In less time than it takes a supercomputer to execute a million penny trades, Jane was skittering on the icy stoop, gripping the rusted handrail to avoid plunging over the side onto the snowdrifts and cobblestones below.   Oh shit. Getting her bearings she realized that no easy way down awaited her. The stoop was a mere balcony without stairs or ladder attached. Pressed for time and without further consideration, Jane went over the side, grasping the iron balusters as she dropped and swung free. For a brief instant she dangled, swaying, in mid-air. A broken ankle would be really inconvenient here, she reflected, trying to gauge the depth of the snow beneath her.   Somewhere overhead someone had begun shouting. Presumably Howie and Bernie, discovering their bird had flown. And also that somewhere along the line their pockets had been well and cleanly picked. Game on, assholes, Jane grinned. And let go.

Once on solid ground, she picked her way with fair speed along the blind backsides of several more shops before finding and ducking up a jagged alley. The alley spat her out on the high street again, near a blind street musician gamely sawing away at the waltz from "Eugene Onegin." The Davos crowd jostled past, deaf to anything but the wheels in their own heads and the sounds of their own voices. The Gypsy violinist felt rather than heard the two wallets that Jane dropped into his open violin case, but he stopped to feel for the bills that fluttered in her wake. *"Nais tuke!"* he called after her, in Romany.   ["Thank you!"]

Bobbing rapidly around and through the knots of paparazzi and their celebrity prey, Jane thrust a bulging money clip into the breast pocket of her topcoat and cursorily examined the Blackberry that Bernie by now was missing.   Behind her, the cocktail hour hubbub reached a new crescendo as Bernie and Howie stood on the sidewalk and threw billion dollar tantrums. They screamed at the shopgirls. They screamed at their goons. They jumped up and down, exhibiting every symptom of spoiled child syndrome.   Seeing the blue lights of a police car careening toward them, the two traders took a minute to shrug themselves back into their camel hair overcoats.   In that brief lull in the action they noticed something odd.

"You're ticking," Howie said.

"So are you," Bernie replied.

A couple of small but satisfying explosions were heard as Jane jumped aboard a passing street tram. The rear of the retreating tram had the last word. 'Think Different' an Apple advertisement recommended, while a Tata poster was still more emphatic: 'Reclaim your life!

14 STRANGE TIMES

Phil's Casket Company was a squat brick warehouse about a block from the waterfront in Yonkers and a world away from the luxury condos that seemed to rise from its roof like glittering fungi, so tall they cast shadows deep into the parking lot even at midday. John stepped out of the taxi and paused to read the sign on the door: "Dying Doesn't Have To Be Expensive."

"Good to know," John said dryly.

The small and seedy front office, crammed with battered furniture and sample books opened to swatches of pink and purple silk and damask, was deserted. So John let himself into the adjoining room, which turned out to be a huge cavernous showroom for a dizzying array of burial paraphernalia – coffins, urns, burial vaults, monuments, all in miniature for display purposes, small enough to fit your average munchkin comfortably. The area was set up like a library or bookstore, the wares on shelves, the shelves divided into sections: Hardwood, Metal, Kosher. John found Vinnie in the Super Economy aisle. He raised his arm in a half-wave as Vinnie spied him.

"So I hear you can get a Star Trek burial, with a U.S.S. Enterprise casket or an urn shaped like Spock's head. Is that right?" Vinnie winked at John.

The elderly woman waiting on him barely batted an eye. She didn't even stop her knitting. Just looked at him over her granny glasses.

"I believe we do have a catalog. Original series or Next Generation?"

"Aww. Can you even ask?" Vinnie said.

She nodded, zooming away in her electric wheelchair. "I had such a crush on Captain Kirk."

"We all did," Vinnie assured her, as he shook hands with John. He looked around for Jane. "You take my advice? You seem to have lost about 110 lbs." John shook his head. "Yeah, well, I still say you should reconsider this reconciliation thing, my brother. You know she shot the balls off her last significant other."

"Urban legend," John insisted, with the ghost of a grin.

"Hey – turns out you CAN make a candle out of earwax. But I digress."

"Sorry about your moms, man."

"On the upside," Vinnie said, "she doesn't have to watch her son become the total loser we always knew he could be."

"They cut you loose too?" John was surprised.

"Minus the use of deadly force, but yeah. "

"Because of us? Because…" John waited for Vinnie to fill in the blanks.

"Like I said, minus the deadly force, so I'm guessing no. No, definitely no, because this was across the board. Flat on my keister two months now. Subspace chatter says some kind of hostile takeover. 'The Firm,' it seems, is now 'The Family.'"

"Sounds cozy and dysfunctional," John said.

"A lot like shock therapy," Vinnie nodded. "A bottom-line reorg they called it. Apparently we cost too much."

"Hell, they already had us on a contract basis," John objected.

"That was outsourcing. THIS is offshoring. Keep up!"

"Whoa. Wait. They can't do that. This stuff – they have to keep this stuff domestic. You don't want foreign nationals running around doing our dirty work. That's – un-American!"

"Nugatory, rubber duck. National security is no longer job security. We've been downsized, privatized, streamlined, and globalized. I've heard it's a total business-to-business operation now, all done by computer. They put a job out for a bid to pre-qualified non-governmental parties and the lowball wins. Some of those South of the Border types are putting a hurt on us old timers; those muthas kill their dear old abuelas just for fun. Or for hassle-free drug-trafficking. No money down."

"One hand sliming the other," John said with disgust. "But speaking of contraband..." He gave Vinnie the box of Cuban cigars.

"Oh Pancho!" Vinnie said, deeply touched.

"Oh Cisco!" John rejoined, helping Vinnie light up. "U.S.S. Enterprise. Really?"

"Yeah," Vinnie says, puffing away. "When I go, I just want them to beam me up..."

15 LAST TRAIN

One other seat at the rear of the car had its overhead light on, but that seat was empty. Finding herself in sole possession of first class, Jane decided to see if Bernie's Blackberry would work after 10 p.m. on the last train to Zurich. Turned out it would - and was not password protected. Bernie, Bernie, Bernie. Jane just shook her head. John didn't pick up, so she called Gerald.

"Sorry to be the bearer of bad tidings, my dear, and hoping you're not going to shoot the messenger," Gerald began.

Jane stopped breathing, fearing the worst. "That can't be good. Spit it out. Is it John?"

"Oh heaven's no. Nothing of the sort. It's just your SBA paperwork has gone missing again. So we're going to have to start over on the loan. Again, I'm afraid."

Jane exhaled. "How many times does this make?"

"Yes, I know. It's really becoming something of a royal pain. It's all being handled by private banks now, you see. They don't let government do anything any more and as far as the banks are concerned it's really so much more convenient to collect the processing fees and just keep their money, don't you know."

"And you call yourself a Tory," Jane teased.

"Humph. I don't know what to call myself any more. But this is Uncle Sam we're talking about. Efficiency of the market and all that.

Amazing what you Yanks put up with. My clients would cut me up for spare parts if I tried that on."

"All I need is a name and a social," Jane offered.

"My dear, don't tempt me," Gerald implored.

"Well, go ahead and try it again, I guess. Maybe five time's a charm. Or is it six? But don't tell John. It's probably a screwy idea anyway."

"He won't hear it from me," Gerald promised. "One more thing before you go. If you get a chance to stop by Switzerland or Monaco while you're out and about, you might want to dip into your safe deposit box and send me a little something on account. Even fake credit cards have to be paid once in awhile. *Ciao*, Bella."

Over her shoulder, a smooth and dangerous voice seemed to echo the words that no one else could have heard. A smooth and dangerous man slid into the seat facing hers.

"*Ciao*, Bella. Where's your other half? In a coma? Six feet under? Or are you having him stuffed for over the fireplace?"

Totally unperturbed and without taking her eyes off the Blackberry, Jane calmly set about deleting her calls from the call log.

"James. *Quelle surprise*. How're they hanging?"

"I get a phantom twinge every now and again. Yours?" James riposted.

"Solid brass. Never better." She made a move to place the Blackberry back in her purse only to have James lean forward swiftly and intervene. He searched her purse with the thoroughness of long practice and, finding no weapon, sat back. Jane cocked her head at him quizzically as he relaxed and resumed the conversation.

"Glad to hear it. I have a little project I'm recruiting for." Jane eyed him measuringly. "I'm waiting for the laugh track," he prompted.

"I'm listening."

"No questions? Comments?"

"You haven't said anything yet."

"That's not usually a prerequisite."

"OK, I'll bite. Public or private?"

"Joint venture. Though in this case government is the junior partner. But I have to ask you again – where's Mr. Doe?"

"Whence this new found obsession with spouses? Once upon a time I might have found it charming."

"And now?"

"Irrelevant." Jane raised her chin and spoke with icy precision. "At the moment Mr. Doe and I are following our separate destinies."

"Sound marital policy," James nodded approvingly. "Very post-modern of you. This is a long-term assignment heading up a new risk-management bureau. Triple the top GS-15 rate, full bennies, plus expenses."

Jane raised both eyebrows and took a shot. "The great right-wing conspiracy pays handsomely then."

"We prefer to think of it as the great right-wing synergy. And by the way - that whole left-right thing? So last millennium."

"I'm more interested in that whole price on my head thing," Jane confided with a touch of sarcasm.

"Oh that," James conceded, as they reached the outskirts of Zurich and the blur of lights streaming past the windows slowed and resolved into an urgent Morse code that Jane could not quite read.

16 COLD WIND BLOWING

Standing with Vinnie at the raw edge of a newly dug grave, John could feel the burner in his pocket vibrating. Once. Again. He had to steel himself not to answer it. It was a Duane Reade special and the only other person who had the number was Jane.

As the two cemetery workers left their hearse and began twisting the crank that lowered the white wicker casket out of view, Vinnie turned away. Behind his back John whipped out the phone for a quick look, but he didn't recognize the caller. Bernie Somebody. A New York exchange. Obviously a wrong number.

They were on the wrong side of a broad field pocked with half-melted mounds of snow and bristling with tufts of desiccated hay, slogging back toward a stand of trees along a graveled track against a cutting wind. Vinnie blew his nose.

"This green burial thing. Very cool. No fuss, no muss, no embalming."

"No Feds," John observed.

"Kind of hard to get a Crown Vic this far off the beaten track,"

"The Caddy made it." John cast a quick look back at the hearse.

Vinnie dodged a puddle. "Yeah well, let's not forget about tomorrow. They're all on special detail now, gearing up for the big changeover. Between tight budgets and shifting priorities, it could be you've fallen through the cracks, my friend. Lucky you."

"John L. Doe. 'L' for luck – or maybe Lazarus."

"The letter we should be talking about," Vinnie said, "is 'V.'"

"As in 'V' for vendetta?"

"Don't get ahead of me." Vinnie held up three fingers. "The real reason you and Jane became a problem. Reasons. Vulnerability. Visibility. And Virtue."

John looked at him without comprehension. "Say again?"

They were so engrossed in their conversation they scarcely noticed that their path skirted a homeless encampment where maybe thirty people were living in tents and makeshift lean-tos. The transients were gathered around a series of campfires at that hour and watched in silence as John and Vinnie passed.

"Turns out once you married that particular honey-bunny you instantly became too vulnerable and too visible for our line of work. Not to mention too apt to compare notes and question some of the games going down."

"But, come on, you know neither of us *knew* –" John objected, throwing up his hands."

"Which brings us to the real fly in the ointment - your kill profile."

"What the fuck?" John paused to let a converted bike-taxi peddle past. It had a large white refrigerated box where the passenger seat should have been. "Finger Lakes Food-Not-Bombs" was stenciled on the side of the box. The driver dismounted near the campfires and opened his box to reveal dozens of Styrofoam food containers. A ragged line began to form, unusually quiet children clinging close to their stiff-faced elders.

"I kid you not," Vinnie insisted. "They actually track that shit and everybody gets a score. Your IQ plus your Oscar-Meyer-Briggs plus how many of what type of assignments you accept and complete. Jane, you? Very weird. Spooky weird. Eerily identical. Before we all got canned, someone somewhere leaked a report showing both of you went for the worst of the worst, time after time. Every hit you ever made – clear villains. No gray hats, no heroes of the people. Just very dangerous, very powerful criminal types with no redeeming social value. The dregs of society. Talking about his father-in-law, here. Works at Goldman-Suxx," Vinnie reassured a man who mistakenly assumed Vinnie was speaking to or about him and whose expression said more clearly than words that he was at once shamed and mortally offended.

"Hold on," John tried to get his head around it. "You mean to say we got in trouble for being good good guys? Or bad bad guys?"

"Now see," Vinnie said, "There's your problem, right there. You don't want to over-think these things. As long as you aren't good and dead guys..."

They swerved to avoid a backwoods-looking group of men and women preparing to butcher a bound and shrieking wild pig. Emerging from the woods onto the cemetery's parking lot, they found that their small and intimate funeral party had grown. Vinnie's car was blocked in by three shiny black Crown Vics.

Startled, Vinnie put a hand out as though to steady himself or hold John back. "Yeah, OK, this was going to happen at some point, right? This was totally in the cards. But I wasn't finished yet, amigo."

John seemed totally unruffled. "I told you not to leave those jelly doughnuts on the front seat, man." He shook his head and reached inside his coat. "Good-bye, Bolivia. Hello, Australia."

About this time, a distant rumble that had been building just out of earshot intensified to a deafening roar that resolved visually into a 1969 souped-up Chevy Camaro. It blew in off the highway and peeled across the parking lot, throwing a door open as it screeched to a halt in front of John and Vinnie, effectively cutting them off from the men in black. As the Feds started to get out of their cars, two women in the Chevy fired stun grenades and tear gas canisters to hold them off. Vinnie grabbed a semi-blinded John and pressed his own gun on him.

"Careful with that," Vinnie entreated. "It was Mom's favorite."

"I thought I was Mom's favorite."

"Cut the crap and aim at something non-essential." But John was too disoriented to realize what Vinnie wanted him to do. So Vinnie placed the gun against his own upper arm. "It's true. We always hurt the one we love." He squeezed the trigger and a shot rang out. "Dammit!"

Vinnie pushed John into the car and clutched the spot the bullet had just creased as the Chevy careened away, the two women laying down more flash-bang and smoke bombs for good measure. Vinnie was rolling on the ground, choking and holding his blood-soaked arm when the Feds found him and hauled him roughly to his feet. One car, then another, took off in fish-tailing pursuit. Several agents made frantic cell phone calls while others handcuffed Vinnie.

"What? Oh really?" Vinnie remonstrated. "I all but hand him to you on a plate and this is – THIS – is what I get? Ow! No more Krispy Kreme for you!"

17 I TRAVEL

Per Swiss regulations, the airport was closed by the time Jane and James arrived. The glass façade of the terminals glowed mint green as the taxi dropped them off. The exterior sweep of the Zurich Circle was desolate at that hour. Even the guards and janitors had retreated to inside jobs and stations. James flashed his wallet at the first security kiosk and was waved down the echoing concourse without a second glance. All the shops and concessions locked up at curfew and only a few unfortunate travelers, stranded between flights, dotted the day lounges and waiting areas. James steered Jane toward the charter flight deck. It was quite a long walk. Without the usual commotion of human herds in transit, there were moments when you felt, followed by the sound of your own footsteps and looking up at the exposed conduits and soaring cross-struts, as though you were touring a post-industrial cathedral.

As they approached the last set of escalators, Jane stopped short beside a hall leading to some public restrooms. James looked at her. She looked at James.

"Alright. Alright. Phone and passport." He held out his hand, and, when she hesitated, waggled his fingers impatiently.

"A little trust?" she said.

"Mmmm. Does that work with John?"

Jane flashed a siren smile and made cat eyes at him. "Baby, everything works with John." She leaned in to hand over the goods and whispered in his ear, "Don't be boring."

In the starkly spotless restroom, Jane darted into a stall where she pulled out her wallet and plucked, from among her business and credit cards, a Samsung miniphone. With all the care and precision that such a minute device required and all the haste her companion/captor's vigilance demanded, Jane tapped out the briefest of messages: "@ZRH. Late? Must run by Walmart. ♥" On second thought, she erased the heart symbol and pressed 'Send.'

When she rejoined him, James was playing a game of 'Pirates' on Bernie's Blackberry.

"And down ye go to Davy Jones's locker," James exulted, handing it back to Jane. As they began to climb the escalator, which like everything else had been shut down for the day, she casually dropped the phone over the side into the cylindrical maw of a shining silver waste bin.

"Yes, I wondered why you had the SEC and the Playboy mansion on speed dial," James noted.

"Isn't it obvious? I'm a zombie banker from the planet Lesbos," Jane was looking at the ceiling, the very portrait of detached ennui.

"Now, see," James admonished, "You say that like it's a bad thing…"

18 LIFE DURING WARTIME

Flying up back roads headed north through the gathering dusk in the front seat of the Camaro, John closed his eyes to try and clear his vision. In the tense atmosphere no one was speaking, but before long he was able to recognize his rescuers. Beside him in the driver's seat was a woman he chiefly identified as a member of the wedding - Jane's maid-of-honor, the woman who was her b-fri and co-worker. Or had been, in their previous life. Whitney Somebody-or-other? Behind him in the back seat, leaning forward and biting her lip, was his former techie wizard Jen. Mousy, prickly, grungette Jen. In a mouse-colored hoodie.

"Ladies! Long time no see." John tried to sit upright.

For reply, Jen crowded him toward the door. "Hold that thought," she said, reaching across him for the handle, "and get ready to jump."

"Next curve!" Whitney warned. She slowed the car from eighty miles an hour to maybe thirty.

"Uh," John started to say.

"Go!" Jen barked. And John went. Followed a beat or two later by Jen. Onto the verge, mercifully padded with brown snow and leaf mold, and down a sloping embankment. The Chevy tore off and disappeared before they reached the bottom. They lay there flat, hardly breathing, waiting for the pursuit cars to rip by. Which they did, within minutes. Like twin beasts, powerful and predatory, the cop cars hurtled out of the gloom, one after the other. Their engines wound to a howl of rage that stopped the heart and lingered in the ear canal long after their taillights had receded.

Comparative silence settled over the countryside and a flock of crows returned to roost in an orchard across the road. John and Jen got to their feet warily and brushed off the worst of the slush and the compost.

"This isn't going to help your career advancement, you know," John said.

"You're welcome," Jen replied, pulling out a nano-flashlight and scanning the ground ahead. "They axed our whole division, including yours truly. By email, by the way. So I'm like - there are no bridges that can't be burned and no porch lights that can't be turned off."

"Hell, I don't even have a porch," John said.

"Yeah," Jen said flatly. She seemed to be waiting for him to say something else. A critter of some kind skittered away in the underbrush. "That - was an eye-opener and a tipping point for a lot of people," she said at last, starting forward through the cordon of ash trees that lined the roadway and keeping her voice low. "When the rectal cranial inversion factor turns homicidal, game over. Besides," she said over her shoulder. "I'm not really here. I'm on my honeymoon. In Iceland."

About fifty feet onward the trees gave way to an open field. John stumbled, narrowly avoided tripping over a furrow. A thin rind of moon was no help at all. The cold was intense.

"Jesus!" John swore, more from surprise than pain. He had not seen the gnarled and leafless shrub directly in his path or the wire connecting it to its neighbor.

"Mind the grape vines," Jen cautioned, shining her flashlight back along the row so he could avoid the trellis. "We're almost there."

'There' was a winery parking lot, almost entirely deserted at this season and this hour, but lit at its center by a lone mast lamp that hummed like a hive of killer bees. In the halo of the lamp, a psychedelic Geek Squad VW bug with DC tags awaited.

"Hell yeah," John commented before climbing in. "We won't be attracting any attention in this baby."

Jen turned the key in the ignition and the bug shuddered to life. "Au contraire, mon frère. This is what invisible looks like. They're scouting for Special Forces types, not four-eyed brainiacs."

From the back seat she pulled a white button-down and a black clip-on tie identical to the ones she was wearing under her hoodie. Dropped them in John's lap.

John examined the shirt dubiously. "What, no pocket protector?"

"Glove compartment." Jen jerked her chin. "Smartass." Semi-amused, John fished it out, plus heavy black-framed glasses and a baggie with what looked like hair in it. He threw Jen a mystified look.

"Soul patch," she elucidated.

John stuck the soul patch on without even looking in a mirror. Taking off his overcoat was no picnic under the circumstances and it was so cold he decided to wear the button down over his Che t-shirt. He caught Jen giving him a quick sidelong look.

"How's your girlfriend?" he asked, trying to match buttons and buttonholes in the dim light of the dashboard.

"You mean my wife? Like I said, we just got married. I left her in Iceland, banging on a can and raising hell about the banks. More to the point – how's Jane?"

"How is Jane?" John struggled to get at his cell phone to see if there was an update.

"Hold your horses, there, Kemo Sahbe. Use mine. GPS disabled." Jen quick-drawed from the hoodie's kangaroo pocket and offered John her handset. He waved her off.

"Who's a noob? It's a throwaway. Uh oh." John scanned the text Jane had sent from Zurich. "Looks like contact has been made."

Jen looked at him aghast. "They've got her?"

"Unclear. She's left Davos and there's some sort of hitch. She didn't use the panic code."

Jen started pounding on the steering wheel and cursing softly in about nine different languages: "Sk?ta, skit, kak, paska, shiesse, and merde!"

"Don't take this wrong, Homeslice, because obviously one of us should be on the verge of some kind of hysteria here, but – what's it to you?"

Visibly upset, Jen gripped the wheel. "Didn't Vinnie tell you anything? Oh my god. I assumed you were in."

John shrugged. "He said – I dunno – we were too good at our jobs. Or some such shit."

Jen stared at him in disbelief. "In what universe does that make sense?"

Looking out the window, John admitted, "I've had that down-the-rabbit-hole feeling for quite some time now."

"Then it's about time you found out what's on the other side of the looking glass," Jen said. She took a deep breath. "OK, here goes."

19 2 + 2 = 5

As Jen began her history, speeding south in the geek-mobile, James was telling Jane a bedtime story over cocktails in a jet somewhere over Germany.

Jen	James
Listen up, boys and girls. Not long ago -	
	Once upon a time, shall we say about forty years ago?
Around the time of the Great Depression -	
	A number of very wealthy people -
A bunch of fucking powerful dudes -	
	Got together and decided -
Looked around and said -	
	You know, things have gotten so screwed up -
This democracy crap is so inconvenient -	
	Wouldn't it be better -
What if we -	
	And they came up with a plan -
OK, was it a plan, was it just how the system came together? The machine...	

It wasn't hard. A think tank here, a trade pact there –

Death of Bretton Woods, IMF, GATT, WTO, Bilderberg, tax cuts, tax havens, corporations without borders, central banks, Glass-Steagall, derivatives, media monopolies -

To set things right -

To really fuck shit up -

And they called it the New World Order.

The goddamn mother fucking New World Order.

Well into French airspace, James paused to survey the five-star entree that had just been set before him. Meanwhile, Jen and John slid into a booth in a Waffle House. Jen continued talking as she perused a syrup-sticky menu.

Jen   James

The deals have all been done -

Actually putting on the finishing touches as we speak -

The trap is slowly swinging shut -

A better world – security, stability, prosperity -

Endless war, extremes of wealth and poverty, a police state -

Her fork suspended in mid-air, Jane raised both eyebrows. "Come ON."

John, equally dubious, could only manage, "Ummmm…"

20 WHEN TWO WORLDS COLLIDE

John cut his eyes toward the unshaven cook framed in the pass-through window and the tired waitress mopping up the counter.

"This is just –" A TV in the corner emitted the Twilight Zone jingle and John pointed to the set. "What he said. Look, it's been – real? But I need to see a man about a wife. And thanks for the get-away."

Jen hesitated, then pushed the car keys across the table. "OK. Go. Just go. We'll call it a scrub." She put her face in her hands a moment and then rubbed her eyes under the glasses she was wearing, exhausted and disappointed. "You're on the list, you know."

"I sorta figured. Tell me something I don't know. Like why."

"I've been telling you why." John made a rude noise. "Look, at some point you're going to have to choose. You don't see it yet, but you will. They've as good as told you which way they think you'll go."

"*They*. I never figured you for a wackjob, Slick." They were silent a moment as the waitress wandered by with more coffee. Jen leaned forward as the waitress went back to filling sugar canisters.

"A superclass of around six thousand. Who control one hundred and forty-seven of the biggest corporations in the world and are maneuvering to own just about everything else on this increasingly hot, crowded, and shrinking planet. Along with the politicians they've bought and the various assorted fucknut fundamentalists, four-star generals, and media whores who support them. And you're not paranoid if they really are out to get you. Why did they try to take you out? Why are they trying to round you up and why do they have Jane? Because if you fall the wrong way, that could be a problem for them."

John gazed at Jen through narrowed eyes. "Oh, really?" He tossed the keys up and down, reflectively.

Jen pulled off her glasses and polished them with the end of her tie, squinting through the grainy overhead light to see if they were really clean.

"Just sayin'…" she said.

21 GOOD NIGHT, BAD MORNING

The jet touched down at Dulles about an hour before daybreak. When the flight attendant brought their coats, James took Jane's and did the gentlemanly thing as he pressed her for a decision.

"I'm afraid it's judgment day, my sweet," he said, close to her ear. "We need to have a meeting of the minds. Because we're due at a couple of very high-level engagements and I have to be sure you don't pose a danger to yourself or others."

Jane turned her head so that her temple almost touched his lips. "That," she observed, eyes downcast, "would be the definition of insanity."

"That would be a get-into-Leavenworth-free card. Insanity is more a matter of violating societal norms. If you accept the new normal – no problem."

Jane turned to face him as he donned a checkered muffler. "What am I missing? I need a job, but you hardly need my buy-in. You have the world on a string. What's your angle, James?"

"I?" James objected facetiously. "Have an angle? I am but a servant of the people. Or at any rate, a very demanding, privileged, and elite fraction thereof. And I am shocked, yes shocked by your suspicion. Wounded to the very core." For a brief moment he grew serious. "Your departure left quite a hole in our operations. To say nothing of my heart. Did you think you were not missed? I've been to the ends of the earth and back again, and I'm here to tell you – there's no one quite like Jane."

Jane dropped a glove. James picked it up and, in giving it back, took her hand and pressed a kiss upon her naked wrist. Jane did not object.

"I see. Mistakes were made and lessons have been learned." Jane spoke with a blithe tone of unbelief that James seemed to find infectious.

"And order has been restored. The world is our oyster. Nothing but blue skies from now on." The flight attendant opened the exterior door and several uniformed guards entered and stood at attention as James ushered Jane toward the exit. "Did I mention the signing bonus?" he asked pleasantly as he marched her down the steps and through the frigid pre-dawn toward a white Humvee flanked by armed MPs.

22 BLINDSIDED

Having driven through the night, a fatigued and frazzled John and Jen dropped the car at the fringes of a packed metro parking lot. Weaving their way through and against an unusually heavy flow of foot traffic, a massive wave of humanity seemingly intent on flooding into DC, they hiked the short but bone chilling distance to a nearby Arlington coffee shop. Washing up on the doorstep an hour before opening, they were nonetheless admitted by the Korean-American owner, stout, wild-haired, and covered in flour.

"What is it, all of five o'clock?" Jen marveled, rubbing her hands together and hugging herself to restore some warmth. "And cold as a Wall Street bankster's so-called heart. Man, you can tell today is the day."

"Can't really blame them," Nick sighed.

"Let's just say I wish I couldn't. And – mmmm – smells like history is not the only thing being made today. Our friend Nick here is a triple threat, I'll have you know. He hacks, he is one with the coffee bean, and the man can cook."

Nick blushed a little and pursed his lips like a bearer of bad tidings. "Chunky monkey scones."

Jen feigned a swoon. "Some people long for virgins in the afterlife. I just want a chunky monkey scone."

"If you insist on being nutty as a fruitcake, I figure it's the least I can do," Nick said. "What's your poison?" he asked John.

"Large coffee?" John supposed.

Jen spoke soothingly to Nick, "He's being polite." Addressing John she said gently, "Would you ask da Vinci to paint by numbers? Make it a double red eye, light cream. I'll have –"

"Sugar-free caramel macchiato, extra dry, no whip," Nick finished. "Outta here, we deliver." He shooed them toward the kitchen.

Passing rapidly through the kitchen, a blur of stainless steel and cracked linoleum, Jen went straight into the cooler, John on her heels. She swung open a set of aluminum shelves at the rear and hit a button on a nearby thermostat. In response, the back wall slid away to reveal a short staircase leading to an otherwise hidden section of basement.

"Sweet!" John said.

"Panic room," Jen replied.

"North Koreans?"

"Jewish mother."

Jen led the way downstairs to a neat, almost monastic hacker's paradise. As their eyes adjusted to the meager blue light, Nick came after them, bearing steaming hot drinks and a paper bag of scones.

"T minus 20, angelpie," he said.

"We don't have to chase them down?" Jen marveled.

"It's the economy, stupid. They've been cashing in those teaser coupons for over a week. Today is free drink day and – " Nick held up his cell phone, one foot on the stairs, "they already texted their order." He ascended to the cooler and the wall slid closed.

As John gulped and munched, Jen hunched over a notebook computer. One end of the room was set aside for a tidy army cot and plastic storage crates containing regiments of books, CDs, and DVDs.

James Carroll's "House of War" lay open, face down, on the white pillow. The rest of the room was arranged around a series of desks and equipment racks meticulously crammed with hardware, including multiple monitors, hard-drive stacks, a half dozen or so servers, assorted network hubs, wired and wireless routers, bundles of cables, a DJ tower, and a huge flat-screen TV.

"Should I be seeing this?" John wondered aloud, setting down his coffee and picking up the book.

"None of us is getting out alive, Mary Poppins. Check your warranty."

"I've never played on this side of the street before."

"Who has?" Jen said. "We're not in Kansas any more and you can't exactly Google map it. Look, if you're a rat, Nick and I are toast. And speaking of bread..." She stood up and beckoned to John to take her place.

Sitting down, John looked at the screen. Looked at her. Then looked back at the screen. "Is that -?"

"Money? You bet your moral compass it is. Ill-gotten gains in secret bank accounts, to be precise. Easier to show than tell. Ya know what they say – one picture..."

"Is worth a million," John chimed in. "Or a *billion* –"

"Yeah," Jen said patiently. "That all?" She stood poised, waiting.

"Well, it looks like a spreadsheet. Dates, names –" He ran a finger down the left side of the screen.

"3 – 2 – 1," Jen did a NASA countdown, softly.

"Holy fucking shit!" John exclaimed.

Jen signaled a football score with both arms. "Houston, we have liftoff!" She immediately sat down at another keyboard and began typing furiously.

"I voted for that guy. And that guy. Almost smoked that guy." He pointed to the screen.

Over her shoulder, Jen threw him a sweet smile. "And now there they are, all on the same page. Lions - and lamb chops."

"Not to mention elephants and donkeys. Where'd you get this stuff?"

Jen raised one shoulder evasively, "Here and there." Then, deciding full disclosure was the best policy, she admitted, "OK, THIS is copied from the DNI collector system – Department of National Intelligence? Yeah. Which siphoned it off the SWIFT international interbank system - what some have called the Rosetta stone of financial data. Repository of all top echelon business transactions, emails, contracts, you name it."

John ruminated on that. "Soooo - basically what you're telling me, showing me," he amended, "is that the world economy is being run as a vast criminal enterprise?"

"Well, " Jen temporized, "I don't think we have any data on China. Yet. But – yeah, pretty much."

"This is, this is –" John tried to describe the sensation of having your brain explode, but words failed him.

"Incendiary? Seismic? Earth-shattering?" The monitor in front of her began to ping gently and pulse with a green light. "Apocalyptic, maybe? I suppose now would be as good a time as any to say that they traced a copy of THAT through a router at your house. What used to be your house."

John's jaw dropped further. "Wait, wait, wait. What?!"

Jen winced. "Yeah. My bad. On the other hand," she changed the subject with a forced cheeriness worthy of Shirley Temple, "based on the current coordinates of the cell phone that last contacted yours (which I can deduce because it is the only unidentified phone at our current location), I believe I have just located your wife. And burner or no, you really need to disable that GPS."

Almost knocking Jen sideways in his haste to check on Jane, John said roughly, "Remind me to strangle you later. Is she OK? Got a visual? Is it live?"

Jen nodded and rubbed her bruised elbow. "Mere moments away as the dodo flies. In the lap of luxury, I might add. Jacked their security feed. Ah, the joys of mass surveillance in the morning." They watched Jane exit the white Humvee and walk into a very large, very white house.

"Why do I get the feeling that there's a good news, bad news joke in here somewhere?" John asked.

"The good news is, she's alive," Jen replied. "The bad news is, she has somehow found her way to ground zero." She pointed at the mansion on the screen - or what little of it they could see. "New World Order, DC branch. Plutocracy on the Potomac."

"Not laughing my ass off here. That's where your secret society lives?" he managed to look both skeptical and worried.

"More like where they tend to congregate when they're stateside, its political, and they want to avoid the limelight. Financial stuff is strictly NYC. These guys? Much bigger in the 80's. Kind of on a down slope now. Think Mickey Mouse Club for Global Domination. Oh c'mon, lighten up. We're fighting a losing battle here. Supporting a cause that's already lost. What the hell. Have fun with it." She went Cole Porter on him, breaking into song: "We're a worthless check, a total wreck, a flop! But baby if we're the bottom, they're the top. Say 'camembert'!"

Picking up a digital camera, she snapped a picture of a beleaguered-looking John, then turned back to the computer where she opened a new window onscreen and began mocking up a fake ID.

23 POKER FACE

The white Humvee cruised smoothly along the restricted HOV lane, passing mile after mile of cars seemingly stitched together at their bumpers and going nowhere fast in the outer lanes. There was no scenery to speak of. The road ran through an artificial valley monotonously defined on either hand by bland high-rise apartments and nondescript office complexes. After about half an hour the car skirted the Potomac river for a brief forgettable stretch, then lost itself temporarily along Arlington streets and byways, before gliding to a stop at the rear entrance of an imposing Colonial Revival mansion. James came round to help Jane out of the car.

"Good morning, Mrs. Doe." He bowed, gesturing toward the house. "And welcome to another day in paradise."

"I haven't had the first one yet," Jane pointed out, noting the absence of fencing or other external security features. "I can't very well have another."

"Ah, but I am in a position to promise you an endless supply. The old rules don't apply here, you'll find."

Jane paused to study the graceful French doors, surmounted by an ugly black surveillance camera. "Did they take it down?"

"Take what down?"

"The sign," Jane said.

"The sign," James repeated, trying to get her drift.

"Abandon hope all ye who enter here."

James nodded, comprehending at last. "That was the old sign. We've ordered a new one: "Abandon hope all ye who can't get in.""

He ushered her into a largish sunroom that had been converted to a security post complete with monitors, computers, and weapons lockers. Through a doorway leading into the main house, Jane could see uniformed maids and other staff in business attire bustling up and down a long corridor, apparently setting up for a breakfast meeting – laying a refreshment table in the wide reception hall, setting out a coffee urn and china, ferrying stacks of folding chairs into a paneled room. A bittersweet waltz – S*onge d'Automne*? - filled the air with subdued gaiety.

"*Senor Cristobal aqui?*"

James addressed this question to a female guard who was sitting at a desk with her back to the door, listening to Lady Gaga and playing 'Left Behind' on her security monitor. The guard jumped up to snap a salute, the music blaring from her discarded headset.

Can't read my, can't read my
No he can't read my poker face

Jane covertly surveyed the metal gun cabinets, which were not padlocked. James caught her eye and she flicked at a voile curtain dismissively, as though critiquing the decorating job. "I would have gone with the plantation shutters and the M16s, but hey, that's just me."

In the reception hall, a real live butler relieved them of their coats and James guided Jane to an immense wooden door that opened into a room that was half chapel, half library. He gave a peremptory knock and entered without waiting for an answer. A weak and watery light was beginning to fill the floor-to-ceiling windows that looked out on an east-facing front portico, but most of the illumination came from a roaring fire. Before the ravenous blaze stood a tall, shambling, pleasant-faced man in his late sixties.

"Reverend Poe, Jane Doe." The right Reverend Christopher Poe and Jane shook hands. Brisk. Businesslike.

"So you're the little lady who was about to make the big war." Behind Jane's back, James waved his hands in warning; Jane looked quizzically at the Reverend, then turned to look at James, who had ceased his frantic motions, resumed a mask of calm, and taken a seat on a large leather sofa.

Turning back, Jane smiled sweetly and said, "So you're the little man who's about to take over the world."

James leaned on the arm of the sofa and covered his mouth with his hand.

"Heavens," Poe said, looking from James to Jane. "What an idea."

"That's not what you do here?" Jane persisted.

"The only thing we do here is the Lord's work," Poe motioned for her to take a seat beside James.

"Then I'm afraid I don't understand your interest in me. I wonder if you've seen my resume?"

"Well you see it's not about my interest, it's not about me or about you, for that matter. It's about all of us working together in the name of Jesus for the greater glory of God."

"And the guns in the back room?" Jane prodded facetiously, pointing over her shoulder.

"Can you ask? An unfortunate sign of the times. You have already alluded to the fact that we have a special purpose and a special ministry. Our flock includes the very rich and the very powerful from every corner of the planet. Their safety and well-being is of course an overriding concern."

"Of course," Jane murmured.

"Also their privacy. The world being what it is, so endlessly divided and contentious, much of what we do must take place out of public view. To be effective - and to prevent misunderstanding. "

"What happens in Vegas stays in Vegas?" Jane quipped.

When Poe answered, he spoke with an iron deliberation. "What happens in this house - *never happened*."

A clock on the mantelpiece chimed the quarter hour. James cleared his throat and said, "Needless to say, Jane is here because we've agreed to let bygones be bygones. She's ready to rejoin the fold, aren't you, Jane?"

This assurance seemed to please Poe, who instantly reverted to his genial avuncular self. "One big happy family, that's what we like to hear. The husband too, I trust?" His gaze shifted quizzically from James to Jane and back again. James looked to Jane for her answer.

"One big happy family," she echoed, but with just enough irony to earn a sharp glance from James.

Just then, Sebastian Ball, a wooly-headed young agent Jane had last seen tied by telephone cords to a motel chair, stuck his head in the door. Glimpsing Jane, he stopped for a moment, confused. Then he addressed James, "Got a minute?"

James stepped around the door and Poe took the opportunity to seat himself next to Jane. He studied her in silence for a moment. Then said, appraisingly, "Yes. I see. This is the next step. "For he beareth not the sword in vain, for he is the minister of God." You've made the right decision and you can count on our gratitude. And our blessing."

"She?" Jane interjected.

"She?"

"*She* beareth not the sword and so forth?"

"I personally have a fondness for First Corinthians: 'Let your women keep silent,' " Poe remarked affably. Jane's eyes began to sparkle dangerously, as even James could see half a room away. He abruptly ended his colloquy and made haste to rejoin the conversation.   But Poe was done.   "Welcome to the ranks of the chosen, Mrs. Doe."   He rose and made a shooing motion.   "And now you children run along and make sure the trains are running on time.   I see our guests are starting to arrive. And I need to brush up on my sermon."

Through the windows, in the ugly dawn, foreign dignitaries, military brass, and business tycoons of many nationalities, along with their assorted female consorts, could be seen pulling up along the circular driveway in every kind of limousine.   Despite the extreme cold, many gathered in small knots and paused to socialize on their way up the front steps.

Poe had already seated himself at a massive felt-covered desk that had the look and feel of an over-sized pool table.   "We'll have a cozy little chat," he promised, "when things aren't quite so hectic."

24 BRIDGE BURNING

In the hacker cave under Murky's Coffee, Nine Inch Nail's "Just Like You Imagined' clicked on. The room began to fill with eerie dissonant synth chords, corrected by a somber piano, driven forward by a drum intro of astonishing fury, joined at last by fearless guitars in a war against the eternal and the inevitable. Jen stood up.

"They're playing our song."

By no stretch of the imagination comfortable with the situation in which he found himself, John demurred. "Jen, I have to be honest. That," he pointed at the computer displaying the mind-bending financial reports, "could be as bogus as hell."

Jen agreed. "Could be. And the economy is alive and well. And your house is still standing. Look. This is not about conspiracy theory. This is about financial empire, power, and global arrangements. NAFTA? BIS? Yeah, I might as well be speaking Greek." She slung a computer bag over her shoulder and started up the stairs.

"What about Jane?" John called after her.

Jen came back to face him. "Two things. If we don't do this right here, right now, we may never have another chance and what comes next will make the current mess look like a birthday party at Baskin-Robbins."

"That's only one thing."

TO ICELAND, WITH LOVE

"You can see we have enough dirt to do some damage, but it's really only a tiny snapshot of a monster story. Half a bargaining chip is better than none. But it's not enough to shut them down. It's not enough to force real change. Besides," Jen reasoned, "if you're going to sell us out, you might as well have the whole enchilada."

"That the game plan?"

"What? Shut them down? Force real change? That would be the hope. But the idea is to get as much as we can and put it out there and let the people decide. Give 'American Idol' a run for its money next month during sweeps."

"Jane and I did not pick this fight," John said.

"No doubt. I could remind you that Jane's a big girl and, unlike poor geeky me, a tier-one professional. But if you feel the need to run to her rescue, Nick can ride shotgun with me. This isn't a job for Superman. And the medals are going to go to the people who try and stop us," Jen admitted.

John clutched his head in frustration. "This is bullshit! I don't want to get political; I just want Jane back and I wanna find some way to get paid!"

Jen was standing on the top step as he said that. She paused and said thoughtfully, "Well now, that last thing? I may be able to help you with." And giving John one last meaningful look, she hit a button to open the sliding wall, pushed back the shelves and stepped into the light. John waited. One Mississippi. Two Mississippi.

"Oh fuck me," he groaned. And bounded up the stairs after her.

On the floor of the kitchen lay two inert forms, two middle-aged heavy-set men in nothing but their socks and skivvies. Nick was wrapping duct tape around their hands and feet. Then one by one he hauled them over to a laundry hamper on wheels, stood them up, and tipped them in. "Sweet dreams."

Jen pulled on a discarded company jacket and a gimme cap, both of which bore a corporate logo – a sort of iron gate - and the words

'Chertoxx Group.' John picked up the other jacket and cap and they walked quickly out to an idling van. White, with the Chertoxx Group logo on all sides. Jen had a hard time exiting the parking lot. Traffic was bumper to bumper. Finally they got a break.

"Who the hell gets up at this hour?" John marveled.

"Welcome to the resistance," Jen said, with mock pity. "You do know what today is?"

"I'm unemployed. Things tend to run together."

"Well, we picked today for a reason. All eyes will be directed elsewhere. And since low people in high places will be biting their nails until the work we – or rather they – were supposed to be doing gets done, we should be able to breeze right on through without anybody giving us a second thought."

"The work they were supposed to be doing. As opposed to the work we will actually be doing." John closed his eyes and leaned back for one exhausted moment.

"Roger that," Jen confirmed. "They were supposed to be upgrading a small but highly hush-hush computer system to comply with new encryption standards, thereby placing its legally questionable, taxpayer-funded software and data outside the public domain forever. Instead – " she fished in her chest pocket and held up a thumb drive. He opened one eye. He could see that what she was holding was a) miniscule and b) embellished with a piratical skull and cross-bones. She clipped it onto the key ring securing the van keys, "- we will be liberating a shitload of incriminating evidence."

"No shoot 'em up bang-bang?" John wondered, both eyes closed again, beginning to relax a little.

"Not if things go according to plan. If they go south, I'm betting you'll be the one to make it out. By any means necessary. Otherwise, you're mostly window-dressing and moral support."

"As long as I don't have to wear heels," John said drowsily. "Sounds easy enough."

"Uh-huh," Jen agreed grimly, turning into the Pentagon parking lot and fumbling on the dashboard for the parking permit the MPs would ask to see. "Piece of cake."

25 HIGH AND DRY

"When's the meeting start?"

"Any minute now."

"Aren't we headed the wrong way?" Jane asked brightly, as James led her away from all the action toward the house elevator.

"Orientation," James said. "Forms, policies, updated background check, blah blah blah. You're not missing anything. The rev doesn't handle the big fish any more. Today he's the consolation prize for a bunch of small fry with outsize egos who don't qualify for the main event. Elites from less developed countries. Cape Verde, Moldova, Panama." The inside of the elevator was paneled with dark walnut. Like a church pew. Or a coffin.

Jane displayed no fear when the motion was distinctly downward. "Ever get that sinking feeling?" she said, pretending to ignore the fact that James was standing far too close.

"They have pills for just about everything nowadays," James said as the elevator stopped.

"Better non-living through chemistry," Jane said. The doors parted and two armed goons reached in. "Hey!"

"Well waddaya know," James threw up his hands. "Conventional wisdom craps out again." He continued to talk as Jane was dragged to a cell, placed in manacles, and hoisted into a stress position. "Turns out you can fool all of the people all of the time. It's the big lie – they never see it coming."

"Nice," Jane snarled. "Family values?"

"Now I'd like to point out that, despite my personal feelings to the contrary, I really have been doing my best to get you and John Boy back together."

"We're such a cute couple. Hey!" Jane said, as one of the guards did a pat down. An NFL ref would have flagged him for unnecessary roughness.

"But so ill-fated. Romeo and Juliet, Anthony and Cleopatra – "

"Smith and Wesson?" Jane interjected. She eyed her surroundings. The arched ceiling, concrete walls, chaste cot. "I see you went traditional down here too. Good choice. Prison-industrial chic really only works in a gritty urban setting. Or a concentration camp."

James was pacing back and forth. "And all because you could not leave well enough alone. What on earth were you thinking? That material was marked 'Burn BEFORE Reading."

"And if I say I have no idea what on earth you're talking about?" Jane said in absolute honesty.

James weighed her denial. "Mmmm. Not the most likely scenario. Doesn't even make the top five. But hang in there sweetheart, we'll sort it out." He waved good-bye and was almost out of the cell when he snapped his fingers. Returned to pick up the handbag Jane had dropped in the tussle. "Almost forgot." He rummaged in the bag. "Ah." Withdrew her wallet and extracted the miniature cell phone hidden there. "Don't you just love Spygadgets.com?"

"Amazing what you can get online these days," Jane concurred. "Plastic flamingoes, vintage Gucci, pre-owned guillotines."

James grunted. He was concentrating on tapping out a message. "I wonder if you really do know what John's been up to? For instance, what would you say if I told you we just located him in the very last place on earth he should visit if he's pure as driven snow? Ah well. I'm on my way to the Pentagon to pick him up. We should be back shortly. Shall I send him your love? One heart or two?"

26 THE KIDS DON'T STAND A CHANCE

The true nature of their undertaking began to dawn on John.

"Are you out of your freakin' mind?" His voice may have risen an octave or two.

"Easy, Farinelli." Jen twisted in her seat to see what exactly was in the back of the van – cables, connecters, 3-ring binders, testers, analyzers. She twisted back. "Thought for the day: 70% of the people in that building are private contractors. They don't work for you and me; they work for the multi-nationals. This ain't your daddy's Oldsmobile."

"OK. This is me minus the Little Mary Sunshine act. I have been playing along just in case this was some kind of FUBARed re-employment test, but it is clearly time for cooler heads to prevail."

Jen glanced at him and hopped out to open up the back of the van, where she pulled a manifest, checked out some disks and documentation, picked up a roll of cable and put it over her shoulder. "Grab that toolkit, how 'bout it? We probably won't need it, but you'll look a little more official and it's got lots of pointy things. Oh – and unpack the heat? That could be a showstopper."

One after another, John took out two guns, his own, then Vinnie's, and dropped them into a box in the back of the van. Then he slammed out of the vehicle and confronted Jen. "You can't just waltz into the Pentagon."

"We'd need a few more for a conga line. This your first time, Captain Doe?" She grinned and slipped him the fake ID. "Don't worry, I'll be gentle."

"Hilarious. You know very well I am NOT popping my cherry here, which is how I know you cannot be serious. If you go in there and you do this-" he lowered his voice and spoke through clenched teeth, "- it's *treason*."

Jen answered him with the clarity of a kindergarten teacher. "So it was just OK for them to put a hit on you simply because they thought you were on to them? And it's OK for them to throw people out of their jobs and out of their homes simply because they have managed to hi-jack the economic machinery? Is it treason to expose treason? I submit to you that everything, literally everything is fucked up. And somebody somewhere has to unfuck it. From where I'm standing, it looks like somebody somewhere has to do something a little bit wrong to prove that a whole lot of other people are doing something a whole lot wrong. Maybe you don't want to be that guy. Maybe I don't want to be that guy. But somebody has to." She beamed at him angelically. "In short, one man's traitor is another woman's whistleblower. And I don't have to tell you the cameras are rolling, so do me a favor and smile like a big dog and just keep walking."

John kept walking. "For the record? This is pure batshit crazy."

"Einstein said the definition of insanity is doing the same thing over and over and expecting different results. Could be you and I are the last sane people on the planet."

"Why don't I find that reassuring?"

"Look. Everything is totes cool. "

"Totes?" John's sarcasm was multi-layered.

"Totes. They are expecting two guys and two guys are showing up. More or less. There will be two passes waiting for us at check-in. Security will call the target office and an escort will show up to take us to wherever they're hiding this very interesting little box of horrors. I'll do my magic, I'll discover – oh no! – we left something critical behind and badda-bing! We're outta there before the first shift finishes its second cup of coffee."

They approached the building as the lights in the vast parking lot were fading out like so many dying stars. They joined a growing throng of employees, both military and civilian.

"And this is supposed to save the world, huh?" John groused.

Jen scrunched up her face. "Gives us a shot? At the very least we'll afflict the comfortable, comfort the afflicted, and get set for some serious Robin Hood action. And, hear me now -" she lowered her voice a little. "If this thing bolos, my advice to you is to double back and come out on the other side. Like Vinnie. You have my blessing."

"Oh right! No blood, no foul?" He addressed the pale impassive sky. "Man oh man. Can we just go back to the good ole days? The drug-lords, the gun-runners, the penny-ante dictators. Life was so much simpler. I was happy."

"Plausible deniability," Jen murmured as they inched toward the south entrance. "It's what's for breakfast."

Two members of the Pentagon Protection Force checked their kit, took their paperwork and fake IDs, and consulted the day's roster. One of them made a quick phone call.

"You're early. They may not be in for an hour or more. No – wait." He spoke into the phone. "Your party's here. Sherlock? Chertoxx. Yeah right." He held out the roster and pointed to a line. "Sign here. Have a seat over there. He'll be up in a few."

John and Jen took a seat on a nearby bench, watching the slow flood of uniforms and suits build and ebb and build again. Shortly thereafter a middle-aged Brit with a phone to his ear walked up, signed them in, shook hands, and gestured for them to follow him while he continued his conversation.

"Oh yes, for an arm and a leg. And we complain about the national health. Well you know, like everything else on this side, falling apart. No, no, I want you to make an appointment and I'll bloody well fly back and have it bloody well done over there."

The Brit led them up passages and down passages to the Mezzanine level, where he carded them into a suite of offices identified by a number and a nameplate that read 'Cascade Systems, Ltd.' The door locked with a decided click behind them.

"No," the Brit nattered on. "Because they won't, that's why. Because it's all a bloody scam over here, a total bloody scam, they only cover you if you're NOT sick. Crazy? Don't you believe it. It's financial genius, love – you come down with something and nine times out of ten they discover, Crikey! It's not an illness they have to treat because you were going to get it anyway. A pre-existing condition they call it. Of course it's ballocks. You bet your sweet Adeline. It's total bloody ballocks..."

He punched a code into a keypad to unlock one of the inner offices, switched on the lights, indicated they should enter, waved encouragingly, and retreated to another room to complete his transatlantic call. Jen looked at John and raised her eyebrows. Archly. Then bent to examine the hardware before them.

"How lucky is this," Jen marveled. "The setup is way old. No cameras, no microphones. But just in case, better rig for silent running," she held her finger to her lips, then swiftly set up shop, plugging in the Jolly Roger flash drive and rebooting to access the root directory. John shook his head doggedly.

"We need to can the window-dressing bullshit. If I'm in, I'm in. You got some 'splainin' to do, Lucy."

Jen sat down, pursed her lips, and thought a minute. "Fair enough. You remember in class how we covered the reporting function?" John nodded, recalling what he had seen onscreen in the hacker cave. "That data was aggregated from sites all over the world. Central banks, private banks, tax havens, investment groups, holding companies. But it had one thing in common. It could all be traced to the same source." She patted the master computer. "What you saw was output. The data this puppy is designed to track, filter, and store. But there is also input. The supply side so to speak. This hard drive literally holds the keys to the kingdom. Routing and account numbers, passwords, IP addresses, stock transaction codes, government contract identifiers – all deemed sensitive, suspect, potentially dangerous or potentially useful to the powers that be. This system, its programs and files, will enable us literally to map the world's illicit money rivers. Like old-timey prospectors and explorers, we will be able to follow every river upstream to its headwaters. In the end we will know not just who's who and what's what - but how it all fits together."

Jen slid a CD out of her computer bag and inserted it into the disk drive. In the outer office the Brit was singing 'Rehab' and trying to make coffee.

"Oh bloody hell. So typical, bloody cow." He stuck his head around the door. John and Jen froze in place. "Damn secretary forgot to restock the tea caddy. She's off today, gone to see the changing of the guard. So I'm just going to trot 'round to Starbucks. Back directly." He walked away. Then, before reaching the outer door, he stopped dead in his tracks.

"Hold on," he said sternly. And came back. Peeking around the door again, he found they had not moved a muscle. "Want anything?" he asked hospitably.

They shook their heads in unison, exhaling in unison when the outer door clicked shut. Jen's fingers flew over the keyboard. John began to prowl the small space like an animal sensing an impending earthquake. He bent to examine a notebook computer sitting atop some other equipment.

"Huh. This looks pretty state-of-the-art." The computer unexpectedly flipped on and mirrored back a picture of him bending down. Next to the video image were two camera stills stacked one above the other – visible wavelength and near infrared scans of his left iris. John had one question for Jen and he asked it in a voice of foreboding:

"How long is this going to take again?"

27 WHILE ALL THE VULTURES FEED

Strung up by her wrists in the basement of the mansion, Jane assessed her situation. Camera over the door, check. Guard posted outside, check. Manacles – she yanked hard this way and that to test them – manacles secure, check. She decided to go for the weakest link.

"Hey there, handsome. Yeah, you." The guard looked over his shoulder through the open door. "Been here long?"

The guard shrugged. Faced forward again.

"No English? No problem. I just thought we could maybe chat or something."

"I have English. You Americans always assume everybody is uneducated like you," he filled the doorway and he was angry. Angry at her imagined insult, angry at the adopted country that had no heart for him, angry at a world that lied about everything. "Exactly how much Somali can you speak?"

Jane bowed her head. *"Waan fahmay. Hal luuqad marna kuma filna."* ["I understand. One language is never enough."]

"Af Soomaaliga maad ku hadashaa?" he said, unbelievingly. ["Do you speak Somali?"]

She nodded modestly. *"Wax yar.* Enough to get around Mogadishu." ["A little."]

He began to look both animated and admiring. About this time, the intercom lodged high up in one corner crackled to life and the Reverend Poe's voice filled the air.

"Ladies and gentlemen, heads of state, captains of finance and industry, distinguished military guests, brothers and sisters all, I want to welcome you to an unprecedented joint meeting of our Foreign Relations and Global Commerce Councils, held on this momentous day, the 20th of January, in the year of Our Lord Two Thousand and Nine."

After the first few syllables, a hand, attached to someone otherwise unseen, stretched slowly slowly slowly from behind the door jamb and applied a stun gun to the guard's neck. Rudely jolted, the guard jerked in a violent spasm and crumpled to the floor. Sebastian Ball, he of the wooly-head, entered and swiftly unlocked the manacles, tossing Jane a cream-colored burka as he strode back to the door.

"I thought that was you," Jane said, rubbing her wrists.

"Well it's not. We've got five minutes," he said. "Ten tops. After that, someone is bound to notice the cameras are all switched to the big meeting and the big boss."

The big boss, meanwhile, was warming up the crowd. "Remember the words of the Pharisee: 'I am glad I am not as other men.' And I say unto you, my friends, that I am glad you are not like other men and women."

Sebastian pulled Jane, who was struggling with the burka, into the elevator. As the elevator rose, he handed her the guard's 9 mm semi-automatic. In the background, Poe could be heard droning away.

"Do me a favor," Sebastian said, "and try not to use that. These guys are so invisible and so connected, the whole security setup is more bling than bad-ass."

"Because after over thirty years in the wilderness, thanks to you, a network of friends from around the ever-smaller world, our mission has passed yet another milestone and we are this very day another step closer to achieving the end we all so dearly desire." Poe coughed and could be heard taking a drink of water.

Sebastian signaled Jane to stay put and stuck his head out of the elevator to reconnoiter. The desk guard had just returned from a quick jaunt to the local Cinnabon and dry cleaner. From the sunroom, she saw Sebastian make a face and draw back into the elevator and felt compelled to investigate. Peering into the elevator, she beheld Sebastian, glued to the rear wall with his hands in the air, mouthing the word, "HELP!" The guard looked puzzled. Reverend Poe's sermon resumed.

"Each and every one of you is here for one reason and one reason only. Because you have shown yourselves to be members of the Lord's elect, and, as the scripture says 'Will not God vindicate his elect?' I tell you, not only will he vindicate them – he will reward them. As you very clearly see in your own lives. You do his work and he rewards you. It's just that simple. A contract. A covenant."

The guard stepped into the elevator and Jane grabbed her, making sure to cover her mouth to muffle any noise. The elevator door slid shut. Reverend Poe pontificated on.

"In proof of that covenant he has given you dominion over all the earth and all the good things in it. Coming from every part of the globe, places utterly wretched, filthy with poverty, wracked by disease, why are you the richest of the rich, why are you the most powerful of the powerful? Because God has ordained it to be so. Because God himself in his infinite wisdom has placed you on the thrones at the top of the world. For 'the powers that be are God's.' Can I have an amen?"

The elevator slid open and the semi-nude guard could be seen slumped to one side, her head pillowed on Jane's discarded clothing. Jane fastened the belt of the black fatigues she had purloined from the unconscious guard, thrust her arms into a leather bomber jacket, and bent down to lace up a pair of combat boots that almost fit. She straightened with two guns in her possession, one from each downed guard. An impatient Sebastian pointed to the burka, discarded on the floor. Jane frowned. "Wanna blow my cover?" he insisted. "We're outnumbered as it is."

"We who?" she whispered in urgent if muffled tones from somewhere inside the burka, which was about as easy to put on as your average long-sleeve tablecloth. But Sebastian was already heading for the back door, where a cab was idling. He had his hand on the doorknob before he noticed something odd. He was escaping alone.

28 JANIE'S GOT A GUN

A few steps from the elevator, Jane had stopped stock-still to listen. And there she stayed, oblivious to Sebastian's increasingly hysterical gestures.

"Of course we have our burdens. The poor we have always with us. But it does keep labor costs down, and over time we have learned how to deal with them. Promise your huddled masses the kingdom of heaven and a shot at the lottery and they ask no more. Over time we have taught them to want less and they are growing ever more content with their dwindling lot and turn on each other before they think to turn on us. Poor in the eyes of the world, they are rich in the faith we have given them."

Sebastian returned stealthily to Jane's side to point at the ranks of limos lining the front drive and the body guards milling all around them, trying to impress on her the need for a quick exit. He tried pulling her in the opposite direction, but she shook him off and stood her ground.

"The same goes for our brothers-in-arms. As the wider society fails, we are careful to promise our military the best of everything. And to shower them with such extravagant praise that they believe our every word and willingly die for us again and again. And I ask you – what would we be without them, our warrior class? With their help we have succeeded in emptying the wealth of nations into our own private pockets. With their help, we have made endless war a way of life. Again, for us, a most profitable state of affairs."

At this point Jane took out one of the pistols and double-checked to make sure the magazine was fully loaded.

"And when in the coming months we begin the next phase of our great work, we will once again call upon our armed forces, those who work for our governments – and those who work for us more directly. I am speaking of our private armies. Our very own Praetorian Guard. With their help we will cease fighting across borders amongst ourselves and turn instead to pacifying internal unrest and maintaining order and stability from the top down. So that all that remains of glory and riches shall belong in our houses forever. To the least acre of land, to the last drop of water." By this time Jane had crept close enough to peer into the conference room, so she could see Poe making the sign of the pyramid, placing the tips of his fingers together, then folding his hands as though in prayer. "As the good Lord intended."

The room was large, spacious enough to seat fifty or so dignitaries with ease. It was a mirror image of the library on the other side of the reception area, except the walls and trim were painted in shades of cream and the sofa, almost lost in the sea of folding chairs, was covered in chintz. Poe stood before a lectern at the far end, facing the door and the dignitaries, directly beneath the second of two period-appropriate chandeliers. Jane noted with approval the numerous etched glass globes and crystal pendants poised like an over-sized papal crown above Poe's head. As the good Lord intended.

"I know," Poe said, "that many of you have had concerns of late. You have shared with me your deepest fears. That the financial Armageddon we unleashed upon the world last autumn would be our downfall. That the election just passed would spell our doom. That our designs would be revealed and our God-given rewards wrested from us before they were safely in our grasp. You will remember I told you all to fear not – fear not. For we are become the very lords of creation. It is we who create the culture, and the law, and the money. In short, everything is within our power. And most important of all – the Lord is with us. Let's be clear. The Lord is on our side. In fact, it has come to pass that there is no other side. As the next few months will irrefutably prove. Verily I say unto you – we are all on the same side now, all working for the same good and the same God. At long last we are all – one. E pluribus unum. At long last, dear friends, we see with the same eyes and we can all see the same God, his kingdom come, his will be done on earth as it is in heaven."

Here, Poe raised his eyes to the ceiling and spread his arms wide.

"Excuse me." Jane's voice interrupted the sacred void at the end of Poe's speech. "Is this the class on 'Speaking Truth to Power?'"

Standing in the doorway, two Berettas poking out of the burka, Jane squeezed off multiple rounds. Most of the august and portly crowd hit the floor, though one or two drew concealed weapons and added to the mayhem by returning fire. With minimal effect and less accuracy, as luck would have it. Jane's aim was true though, and one after another the lovely glass globes exploded, sending a rain of tinkling shards down upon the right Reverend Poe. A final shot neatly severed the chain of the chandelier, which hurtled toward Poe as though it was the avenging needle's eye and he the proverbial camel.

Sebastian, meanwhile, had triggered the panic doors. As alarms rang out, he caught Jane from the side with a flying tackle, knocking her into the hall as the bulletproof shields slammed into place.

Men with guns streamed in from out of doors. Fortuitously, more shots and screams were heard within the conference room. Helping Jane up off the floor, Sebastian shouted over the pandemonium: "Some nutcase started shooting and we're on lockdown. We need to evacuate ASAP, let's go, let's go."

Leaving his associates to deal with the situation he had helped to create, Sebastian bundled Jane toward the sunroom and the cab. With everybody else otherwise engaged and the gun cases hanging open, Jane grabbed an AK-47 and a box of clips as Sebastian locked the interior door between the sunroom and the rest of the mansion, jamming a chair under the doorknob for good measure. Next he grabbed the desk phone and held it out to Jane.

"I think you know what to do with this."

She took it with a smile, saying, "Here's looking at you, kid." And smashed him across the jaw. He went down like a bad bank stock.

The Pakistani cabbie, who had been standing with one foot on the running board and looking nervously at the house, watched this scene with a dropped jaw. Before Jane could open the door, he jumped into the cab and peeled out.

"Chickenshit!" Jane stormed. She leaned out, surveying the grounds to left and right, about to make a run for it, when, still supine on the floor, she heard Sebastian weakly clearing his throat.

"Ahem?"

Jane looked down to see a set of Vespa keys dangling from his forefinger.

29 SEVEN NATION ARMY

In the Cascade Systems office, Jen was cursing softly.

"Come on, come on. God, I hate Windows. Bill Gates should be hung, drawn, quartered, shot, poisoned, disemboweled, and then REALLY hurt."

John was pacing again. His phone vibrated. "Oh great," he said, scanning the message. "Jane's ex says to sit tight, he's on his way. Playtime is over. Time to un-ass, Sparky."

"All. Most. There. Wiping up. Here." Jen detached the flash drive and tossed it, keys and all, over her shoulder to John.

"I don't suppose I could test drive a cruise missile instead?"

"Yippee-ki-yay, motherfuckers! One for you, one for me." She ejected and brandished the CD.

"That reminds me. As far as escaping goes – is there a Plan B?"

Jen dug into her computer bag and brought out a pad of paper and a ballpoint pen. She scribbled a few words and held it up for John to read.

"Memorize. Got it? Deliver that lowly tchotchke in four weeks or less and you and Jane can look forward to a nice little happy ever after, courtesy of the Forbes 500." She stripped the paper off the pad, balled it up, and stuck it in her pocket.

"With a little help from you and coffee shop guy?" John asked, as the office door closed behind them with a click and they backtracked up the hallway.

"Yeah, I get by with a little help from my friends. I get high with a little help from my friends," she sang. "Can you say – " she looked around conspiratorially at the military personnel passing by, "-Wikileaks?"

John blanched, choked, and glanced around to ascertain whether or not Jen's remark had been overheard. He closed one hand around her upper arm to hurry her along.

"I thought you could," Jen grinned. "The assholes may be rich, but we are many."

The hallway stretched on interminably. Buzz cuts with side arms seemed to come at them from every direction. Trying to project an air of normality, John began talking nonsense. Extras on a movie set are taught to say "Peas and carrots, peas and carrots." He just said the first thing that popped into his head: "Speaking of rich, do you mind if I ask what exactly you mean by a 'nice' happy ever after? Is that like a minimally comfortable but no-frills nice or a fairly affluent bordering on luxurious nice, because Jane – "

"Naughty!" Spoken loud enough to make heads turn, the word brought them up short. It was the Brit, returning with his cuppa and shaking an admonitory finger. "No wandering about. This isn't an amusement park, you two. If you're not careful, the boogeyman will get you."

Jen tugged at the coil of cable over her shoulder. "Needed angel hair, brought vermicelli. Thought it would be faster if we met you halfway."

Before they had gone much farther, the sound of heavy footsteps began to echo somewhere up ahead, approaching in double time. Jen pulled up short and looked at John.

"Aaachoo!" She feigned a violent sneeze. "Achoo, achoo! Oh golly. Kleenex," she said, holding one hand over her nose and plunging into the nearest ladies' room. John's phone began to vibrate. Two rings. Stop. Two more. Jane! He smiled beatifically at the Brit and jerked his head toward the men's.

"Probably a good idea." And he too vanished from view as a squad of military police thudded around a corner.

Having traded the burka for a Bluetooth helmet, Jane was trying to make her way to the Pentagon through total gridlock, dodging between cars, speeding along medians where necessary. She was calling from the congestion and chaos of the freeway. John was listening in the tense quiet of the Pentagon restroom.

"Baby, the traffic is hell, but I can be there in five," she shouted.

Pretending to check out his borrowed soul patch and watching a corporal wash his hands, John asked casually, "How'd you make out at Walmart?"

"About like you'd expect. Scratch that. Exactly like you expected. The inmates are running the asylum. Meet you at the I-395 walkway?"

"Make it the pet store," John said. "You owe me a parrot." The door closed on the corporal, leaving John free to strip off his soul patch, cap, and jacket and stuff them in the waste bin.

"With the whole world crumbling," Jane groaned. And the connection went dead.

"Tell me about it," John said bleakly. He sighed, closed the phone, and stood there tapping it against his upper lip.

He emerged cautiously to find Jen shifting her computer bag from hand to hand. She too had shed her Chertoxx togs.

"I say," the Brit said, putting his head on one side as the tumblers in his brain sought to click into place. But before he could analyze what was wrong with the picture, John said, "Nice tie. Manchester United?"

Instantly diverted, the Brit held up the tip of the tie, where a tiny devil danced with a tiny pitchfork. "Glory, glory, Man United," he sang in a rich baritone. To the tune of Ms. Howe's immortal "Battle Hymn of the Republic."

"We should *all* be marching on," Jen urged, not waiting to see who was following.

"Heard the Chipmunks' version?" John asked and squeaked a few bars. Between laughing and sloshing his tea, the Brit was having a hard time keeping up. They were close, so close to the main entrance. Up one more ramp, into the wider hallway, almost in sight of all the saintly sober portraits of the men who ran the wars. That was when they heard it, impinging at the very edge of hearing at first, but growing unmistakably louder. The sound they had been dreading. The tramp of many boots in unison, coming this time at a dead run. Worse luck, up ahead they could see a bottleneck of sorts, a spot in the corridor where people were pooling up.

"Reminds me," the Brit said, choosing that moment to cross the hall and press a buzzer. "Just need to nip in here and lay a friendly bet on tonight's game. Won't be half a mo'. Arsenal fan," he confided with a wink as the office door opened. Before John had time to react, the door closed and he was staring at a "Restricted Area" sign.

"I don't suppose," John said to Jen in a tone that indicated he tended to doubt it, "you brought us any toys to play with?"

"Life saver?" she asked cheerfully, as they drifted in among a knot of bystanders watching some sort of film being shot. Four generals and a chaplain faced a camera, a boom microphone, and a bank of lights. A sign on an easel reads, "Thank you for being quiet. Faith Embassy Productions." John looked down and saw that Jen was passing him a string-pull smoke bomb masquerading as a roll of Wint-O-Greens. Also a cigarette lighter and the balled-up paper from her pocket. "That's nitrocellulose by the way," she added in a whisper. "And did I mention we've got a taxi waiting?"

"I'm meeting Jane at the mall," John said.

"Shhh!"

A dude wearing a headset and working a movie clapboard leaned backward to see who was ruining the take. He was wearing a white button-down, a skinny black tie, and black-rimmed glasses. Just like Jen and John.

"Oh my god, look. We're Mormons," John muttered.

"SHHH!"

The clapboard dude gave them a decidedly un-Christian look, which John and Jen sought to deflect by shushing the people in front of them. Meanwhile, the officer with the most chest candy burbled on.

"I tell every recruit I meet that it's God first, then family, then country. That we are a nation under God and my faith is at the forefront of everything I do. That's why I have been a Prayer Warrior for twenty years and why I support all the fine folks at Faith Embassy."

"Praise Jesus!" Jen yelled. "Hallelujah!"

30 TURNCOAT

All eyes turned in her direction. Which gave John the split second he needed to drop the smoke bomb in the trash bag of a janitor's cart standing near at hand. As the smoke began to well up, he surreptitiously lit the flash paper, which followed the smoke bomb into the trash bag. Ditto the zippo, still burning.

In the nick of time. The heavy boots and the ten soldiers wearing them chose that moment to burst upon the scene, guns at the ready. WHOOSH went the trash bag. "FIRE!" went John. And made a dash for the nearest fire alarm.

"Here now!" said the Brit, emerging to find the place in total chaos. The fire alarm was whooping, strobe lights were flashing, the film crew was panicking. "Want me to get that?" John asked the cameraman, who was struggling with his equipment. Without waiting for permission, he picked up the easel and the "Faith Embassy" sign. Like ants presented with a more immediate danger, the soldiers automatically regrouped and divided to combat the burning trash bag, flames from which were now shooting up to threaten the drop ceiling. Over the intercom a mechanical voice droned, "Code Red, M-1. Code Red, M-1. This is not a drill, repeat this is not a drill." Offices on every side began to disgorge tens then hundreds of workers, all of whom streamed toward the nearest exit, John and Jen bobbing anonymously in their midst.

They were actually on the pedestrian walkway, approaching the last set of gates and turnstiles when up ahead a cordon of Pentagon police officers in full winter dress marched into position, blocking the way.

"Remember, remember, the fifth in Vesturbaer," Jen chanted and sidled away through the crowd to stand beside a crying child, who seemed to have become separated from a tour group. She caught the child's attention when she took a piece of paper out of her computer bag and began to fashion an origami dove. Sobbing a little less, the child, all princess-pink parka and Pooh-bear backpack, watched in fascination and stuck close to Jen as everyone surged forward toward the parking lot and the buses.

"Deondra! Deondra!" a frazzled woman called, knee deep in Gap Kids on the other side of the solid black police line. Jen handed the paper bird to the little girl, who woke from her enchantment to shriek, "Mommy, mommy!" At which point Jen picked the child up and bore her like a magic talisman straight through the implacable wall of men.

John was going for the Invisible Christian effect. He shifted the easel to his left hand, readjusted the sign to make sure it could be read, and concentrated on sending a text message to Jane with his right. No one challenged him as he shuffled between two figures very nearly as taut and muscled as he was himself. But before he could breathe easier, he felt an arm around his shoulders and a voice in his ear dictating a message very different from the one he had been typing.

"Treason. T-R-E."

"Said the pot to the kettle."

"I," James said virtuously, "am not wanted for murder and espionage in 188 countries."

"And I have been busy supporting and defending the Constitution against all enemies foreign and domestic. So if that's all you've got…"

"What I got," James said, and his words were underscored by the sound of guns locking and loading, as the guards pivoted to train all their weapons on John. "What I got – is you. And our Jane of course. Birds in the hand."

John's gaze wandered over the guns, with whose muzzles he more or less stood eye to eye. "No doubt you're hoping for a silent spring."

"Silence is golden," James agreed.

"Which brings us to the golden rule."

"He who has the gold makes the rules," James said, in no uncertain terms.

"And he who knows who has the gold and how they got it?" John asked.

"Is playing against the house. And the house always wins."

"Maybe not - if it's a glass house."

"You know," James sighed, tiring of the game, "it's a damn shame, but under current law we can't beat the piss out of you on government property. The sooner we adjourn, therefore, the better. Let's move." He signaled to the guards.

Roughly handcuffed and tightly surrounded, John was marched down the walkway through the shivering evacuees toward the south steps. Across the parking lot with its eight thousand cars, across the tangle of intervening highways clogged with traffic going nowhere on that bright winter day, a mere two blocks away as the crow flew or the blameless tourist walked, he could see the facets of the Pentagon City mall blinking in the sun like the world's biggest Zircon diamond. At least Jen had gotten away, and Jane was over there somewhere. Safe. Two out of three. Not too bad, considering...

31 (WE'RE NEVER GOING TO SURVIVE UNLESS WE GET A LITTLE MORE) CRAZY

High atop the Pentagon City parking deck, Jane had received John's truncated message and could see some kind of drama unfolding across the street. Then she watched as the white Humvee detached itself from the south steps and headed for one of the many Pentagon exits, swerving into the lane for Crystal City. That made sense in a way, since almost all the congestion was in the other direction, aiming for DC; but why not back to the mansion? Just how many private little prison camps were these guys running? She put the helmet back on and prepared to give chase. She would have to be quick. The car was stopped at a light and she was five levels up. She gunned the Vespa and was arcing around, getting ready to make the jump to light speed, when she heard someone calling.

"Hey lady!" Jane didn't immediately recognize the glammed-up bombshell in the blonde wig waving at her from the back window of a stretch limo emblazoned with the words "Party Grrrrls."

"Whitney?"

"Are you missing that pretty man of yours again?"

"Funny you should ask. Don't suppose you have a grenade launcher a girl could borrow?" Jane stretched to see whether the Humvee had moved on.

"Well, actually," Whitney said, opening the door to reveal four more of Jane's old team – all in blonde wigs – and a fairly impressive arsenal.

"Oh baby," Jane crooned, unshouldering the AK in favor of a sweet little M4. "Come to mama." She climbed in and the limo purred forward.

"Didn't even have to say 'follow that Humvee,'" Jane marvelled. "OK, are we officially in the Twilight Zone? 'Cause there is no way you all can be here."

"Oh, way," Whitney disagreed, passing Jane a Perrier. "The day after you got 'fired'? We ALL got pink slips."

"Do boys get baby blue slips?" Jen asked from the driver's seat. She was looking oh so official in a chauffer's cap and Ray-bans.

"Tweed maybe," Wallis said.

"A tasteful shade of gray," Willa offered.

Jane narrowed her eyes at Jen, a stranger. "She come with the car?"

"She came with your husband," Jen answered, a tad sharply.

"And apparently lost him somewhere along the way?"

"Take it down, Pussycat. John's side of the family." Whitney put a hand on Jane's knee to emphasize her next words. "LES'-ALL-BE-FRIENDS."

Jane looked from Jen to Whitney and back. Smiled poisonously. "You must be Jen."

"Back at ya, Prom Queen."

"Laadeez –" Whitney said warningly. "We can fight each other, OR – we can fight them? The point is we know what these jokers are up to and we are all in this together."

Jane flounced back in her seat. "Kumbayah already! Now where does that leave John?"

The limo paused at an intersection about half a block behind the white Humvee, which had stopped in front of a twin-towered building with a façade of dark glass. James, John, and several guards got out and immediately entered the building. Whitney pointed.

"Planet Merck. Official non-existent black site."

"Black hole," Jen commented.

"People go in –" Willa said.

"And they don't come out," Wallis finished.

Jane was silent a moment. Stiffening the old backbone. "Alrighty then. Cue the intrepid tiger wife. Thanks for the ride, boys and girls. Don't take any wooden nickels – or any synthetic CDO tranches for that matter." She drew a deep breath and reached for the door handle.

"You think that's how we roll?" Whitney scoffed. "Uh-uh, girlfriend. This is everybody's party."

Jane looked dubiously at the camo miniskirts and cutoffs her friends were sporting beneath long military coats. At least they were wearing Doc Martens instead of four-inch heels.

"C'mon. You are the last person to be played by a pair of hotpants." Whitney held out a pair of scissors as the others strapped on drop leg pouches and loaded up on ammo. And airplane bottles – scotch, bourbon, tequila. Whitney put on her jivest face. "Dey jus' the price of admission."

32 RAISE YOUR GLASS

On the black marble wall between the two elevators, two building directories. One for the left hand tower - American Legislative Exchange Council, Americans for Prosperity, Club for Growth, Council for National Policy, Focus on the Family, Heritage Foundation, Peterson Institute, Voxx News. And one for the right. – BAD Systems, Foeing, KBRU Kidding, Lockhead Martin, Northrop Gunmann, Raypeon, SaICK, and Darkwater USA. Merchants of deceit and merchants of death. Joined at the parking garage.

"One stop shopping," John nodded. "How convenient."

"Minipax, Minitru, Miniluv," James said, pressing the button.

"And you work for –"

"All of the above. Same as it ever was. Never seemed to bother you before."

"What can I tell you, man?" John said, "Lose your job, lose your identity."

On that note, well-known talk-show host Glenn Dreck entered the lobby. In a pink shirt and navy suit, he strode purposefully toward the other elevator. Stopped. Just stood there. James looked over at him.

"Saw the show last night. 'One-world eco-nazi brie-eating climate commie.' Good one."

117

"Uh, thanks. Thanks. You too," Dreck said. He seemed confused. Possibly he was trying to remember who James was. Or wondering what a man in handcuffs was doing in his office building. As James tried to hustle John into the elevator, John leaned over and whispered loudly: "Psst. You have to press the button if you want it to go."

The elevator doors closed, followed by the sound of a sharp blow and a grunt of pain. A red-faced Dreck reached out to press the elevator button. As he did so, he heard a furious knocking sound. He drew his hand back. The knocking stopped. Cautiously, he reached out again and this time he heard banging. Once again he drew his hand back and the banging stopped. He was about to experiment a third time, when he heard the guys at the security desk say:

"Are you serious? Can you see those breezies? No man, no. Just buzz 'em on in. Enough with the Barnie Fife routine."

"That is exactly the attitude that brought us 9/11."

"Now don't you start. What brought us 9/11 was a bunch of oil dudes with long-range plans, short-term greed, and no kind of morality. We should learn from them. Carpe diem. Means 'seize the woman.' Ain't nobody in their right mind going to come in here and make a fuss. They got the whole rapid response team on alert up there. Armed to the teeth. So open that door." A brief scuffle ensued, during which the door did open, allowing Jane and her posse to breeze in.

"Ladeez," Officer Horndog came forward smiling.

"Look out, they've got guns," his partner shrieked, reaching for the phone and his sidearm. "I told you, I fucking told you."

"No no no – no no no." Jane rushed to reassure them. "You've got it all wrong. We're here for the model shoot – Pentagon Playgirls calendar. Isn't that right, Mr. Dreck?" Jane wheeled to appeal to Dreck, who was crouched down beside a shiny black waste can. Behind him, the elevator door opened and then shut again, like a mechanical mouth balked of its prey.

"Hmmmmm?" Dreck stood up awkwardly and straightened his tie. His face was red again, but he came forward willingly enough.

"It's part of your 'Support the Troops' initiative."

"Uh. Oh. Is that today?"

One of the posse was watching the elevator read-out to see where John and company got off.

"Top floor," she reported.

"We're on a tight schedule." Dreck was lost somewhere between her cleavage and her legs, revealed to the upper thigh. She had to bend sideways to catch his eye. "Hope you don't mind. We're going to start upstairs in the," she checked the directory, "Darkwater conference room."

"Mind? God no. I mean, it's all for a good cause, right? Allow me," he waved them toward the elevator. "You have to press the button," he explained, demonstrating with a flourish.

It was a pretty tight fit in there, with six tall, drop-dead gorgeous Snow Whites and one intellectual dwarf. Dreck saw nothing wrong with the picture. He was too busy having a ball.

"It's a calendar? But there are only —" he counted under his breath, "six of you."

"Well, you see," Jane explained, "We're going to do six shots in costume —"

"- and six without," Whitney, Wallis, and Willa chorused.

"Kinda gives a whole new meaning to the term 'Dirty Dozen,'" Jane did her best Mae West impression. Behind her, the girls pulled on night vision goggles.

"Hey!" Dreck yelled, as someone slipped a black silk hood over his head.

"Shhhh," Jane cautioned, as the girls hid on either side of the door. "It's sort of a surprise."

"Ah!" Dreck nodded as the door opened onto the posh reception area of the Darkwater offices. "I see."

33 NEVER SAY DIE

John found himself in a tidy little torture chamber, furnished with a restraint-equipped tilt-table, a tiger cage, a metal chair, racks of knives and other sharp implements, floor and ceiling bolts and chains – everything your state-sponsored enhanced interrogation professional could desire. James watched as John was situated in the chair, earning a fat lip and a black eye in the process.

"Aren't you forgetting the German Shepherd?" John bent double as a guard sucker punched him.

"We actually have one around here somewhere, but I don't have time for stupid pet tricks. I'm late for a really big show. So you have exactly five minutes to spill your guts – or have them spilled for you. After which I will of course turn my full attention to the lovely and recently widowed Mrs. Doe."

"You think?" John smiled. Wagner's 'Ride of the Valkyries' filled the small room. James's phone was ringing, but he chose to ignore it. He had seen John's smile.

"The real mystery is what you think. What the hell do you imagine you're doing? This is not about a few bad apples, you know. This is a system. A system of interlocking systems. You can't beat it. So the question is not – gasp – can we get away with it. We already have. The question is – why fight it?"

John shrugged as his shirt was ripped open and electrodes attached. "Guess it's just the way I'm wired."

"Ha ha," James laughed mirthlessly. His phone rang again. "Pockets!" He snapped his fingers and pointed, indicating that he wanted John to be searched and his possessions confiscated. He pulled his phone out, checked the number, and examined the contents of John's pockets – wallet, phone, keys. He zeroed in on the keys. "Hello. Who are you I wonder?" He detached and examined the Jolly Roger thumb drive.

"Then again," John said hastily, "it could be that this is a triple-reverse sting, meaning your Legion of Doom is busted and you are all going down."

"Right. And the marines will be breaking down that door any minute now. Except they won't. Because we own them too. I'm listening," James said into the phone, which had not ceased its Wagnerian refrain. He was silent a moment, then swiveled slowly to face John. "I hear you. No, the chopper. It's a parking lot out there. Right."

John smiled cherubically. "You were saying?"

34 BAD GIRLFRIEND

In the elevator, Whitney inserted a shiny silver key in the Fire Service lock and turned the switch to 'Manual.' When the door opened on the twentieth floor, she pressed the 'Hold' button, taking the elevator out of service for the other floors. The reception area was deserted except for a couple of salesmen with sample cases and an Ernest Borgnine type manning a glass-encased control center. In the elevator, Wallis started a boombox and the girls all shouted, "Surprise!" and came shimmying out of the elevator, leading the hooded Glenn Dreck by an extension cord. Dancing all the while, they flirtatiously secured the hands of the salesmen with plastic cuffs, then unbuckled their belts and dropped their pants around their ankles. Turning to the control center, they gestured like Homer's treacherous sirens for Ernie to come join them. And he came, earning the reward of a wee dram from an airplane bottle of Grey Goose vodka. Getting into the spirit of things, he willingly accepted his handcuffs and a black hood like Dreck's. Willa stood guard over all the 'prisoners' while the other five began a room-to-room search.

Several of the rooms were unlit and unoccupied. However, the fourth door opened on an ugly scene. One man seated in an ordinary office chair, two men standing. The seated man looked like a mummy getting a shave, his head forced back and smothered by a towel. One of the standing men was doing the head forcing, the other poured water from a carafe in a steady stream onto the sodden towel.

"Free lap dances in the break room! Last one there is a monkey's football!"

"Man, is this place the shit or what?" Carafe Guy held out his wrists with alacrity.

"At the Bureau we're lucky if they order pizza," Towel Guy acknowledged, as Wallis herded them out of the room. They left without a backward glance or second thought for their hapless victim. Whitney immediately jerked the towel off the mummy. Who turned out to be our good friend Vinnie. The wet towel removed, he gasped for breath and bent forward, expelling water from his mouth and nose, coughing and choking.

"Red Ryder Carbine-Action Two-Hundred Shot Range Model Air Rifle," he fell back and gabbled in a whisper. "Ma, ma! I shot my eye out." He recovered enough to recognize Jane. "Oh no. Am I dead?"

"Love you too," she snapped. "Where's John?"

Vinnie pointed at Whitney, "She had him last. You know this probably isn't the time or the place, but a feather boa would go great with that."

Whitney handed him a small packet of plastique, timers, wires, and detonators. "Go make yourself useful. Booby-trap something or other. And tell Wallis to pump up the volume."

The music got so loud the walls began to vibrate. Distracted by the noise, feeling pressured by a situation over which he no longer had total control, and faced with the realization that John was not going to play ball, James vented his irritation: "Jesus. They let the psy-ops guys out again." He went to open the door and was immediately forced backward. The Jolly Roger thumb drive went flying. "What the fuck?"

Jane and Whitney came in low, to the left and right, guns at the ready, followed by Wanda and Wendy. "Freeze! I said FREEZE. On the floor. Everybody down. Especially you, asshole. No faces. I don't want to see any faces." Whitney and the two other women quickly disarmed and restrained the three men. Jane frisked James where he lay and did not come up empty handed.

"Nothing back here. Turn over. Hello." she grazed his belt buckle. "Is that a gun or are you just happy to see me?" she said, holding up a Glock 27.

"This is the side of you I always find so unattractive," James complained, struggling to reach a sitting position.

"The side that can whip your ass? Yeah, I can see where that might be a problem." She went to John and tenderly removed the ball gag from his mouth. He smiled gamely.

"Of all the torture chambers in all the towns in all the world…"

"Your beautiful face," Jane said, touching his swollen eye.

"Eh," John said. "I've been hurt worse. By girls. You for instance."

"Maybe. But I'm still officially pissed." She bent to unbuckle his wrists and ankles.

John stripped off the electrodes swiftly and methodically. "Now Jane honey," he began, standing up and testing his jaw to make sure it was not dislocated. "Remember what the therapist said. Anger isn't always a bad thing. It has a purpose in our lives."

The music changed. From 'Bad Girlfriend' to 'Time to Run.' The other women looked at one another, looked at Jane. Willa stuck her head in the door, singing "Shit hitting fan. That is all."

"Go," Jane waved them away. "Seriously. All the way. Consider that an order. For old time's sake." They went.

John scooped up the guns the girls had collected, tucking a couple into his waistband, but holding onto James's Glock. "If you're threatened or hurt," he continued, as though he had all the time in the world, "anger can give you the energy and motivation you need to straighten things out, make things better. It's when you hang on to rage and feed the hostility that it can hurt you. Would you mind closing the door, sweetheart?"

Mind? I thought you'd never ask." Jane closed the sound-proof door and leaned against it with her head to one side as John wheeled, aimed directly at James's chest, and coolly pulled the trigger.

The shot reverberated and James rocked backward in well-deserved pain.

"Rats," Jane said. "You know? I forgot to tell you. He's wearing Kevlar today. But thank you, darling. When you're right, you're right." She drew a deep yoga breath and let it go oh so slowly. "I feel so much better."

James spoke through gritted teeth. "Congratulations. You just made the record books for worst career move ever."

"Then you won't mind if you never see us again," Jane said, opening the door. "See John and Jane run. Wait – what's that?" She bent to pluck something from the floor. The Jolly Roger thumb drive, which had almost gotten lost in the scuffle. "Oh look! Speaking of pirates."

"I saw it and thought of you," John smiled.

"John," Jane said, as pleased as if he'd given her the Hope diamond. She tucked it into her breast pocket and gave it a little pat. "Good luck charm."

"It was a test, Jane," a recovering James managed to gasp. "And you are failing. You have failed. Both of you. You're done. And that goes for your entire Sesame Street gang."

"I'll get you, my pretty, and your little dog too!" Jane vamped. "I believe that, actually. At least, I believe you'll try. Everything else is a fairy tale."

"Last chance," James warned, watching as his prize pigeons prepared to fly the coop, with his future in tow. "Come clean, let sleeping peons lie, and you can spend the rest of your days hanging out with Ken Lay on that private sunny beach."

"I am so not buying it," Jane shook her head in supreme disbelief.

"And Jane makes all our major purchase decisions," John said.

"Suit yourselves," James growled. "Your funeral."

The music had died to a whisper so it was possible to hear John and Jane quite clearly as they walked away.

"Wasn't it Yogi Berra who said you have to go to other people's funerals or they won't come to yours?"

"It ain't over till it's over."

"Déjà vu all over again..."

35 ENDGAME

The phones were ringing off the hook in the control center, but otherwise the place was a tomb. Jane's crew had left a Post-It note on the elevator and a body in front of it.

"Other kids playing post-office in break room, don't trip over new guy, Vinnie looks great in drag, call me sometime, Whitney. PS - Don't forget to duck @ 11:45."

"What time is it now?" Jane asked. "You know, that guy's paramilitary." She inspected the new guy's body armor. Noted the helmet a few feet off and the goose egg on his forehead. "Where'd he come from?"

"11:44. And they don't travel solo. Stairs?"

At that moment the elevator chimed.

"Uh –" Jane glimpsed more helmets and body armor as the doors began to part. Felt her neck snap as John snatched her past a palm tree, around a corner, and out of sight.

"Mamba Leader One, this is Mamba Leader Five, we have a man down at main base, do you read, over."

John pulled Jane toward the exit sign at the end of the hallway, silently marking time with the muzzle of the Glock. Three, two, one.

It was a pretty impressive blast, given what Vinnie had had to work with. Smoke, alarms, sprinklers, overhead sirens, and flashing lights followed. Glass everywhere. Leaving chaos behind, Jane and John got to the stairwell and started down. Only to hear a door flung open a flight or so below and dozens of men in battle gear headed their way. John and Jane reversed course and scrambled upstairs instead, hiding in the shadows at the very top of the steps leading to the roof. The entire contingent emptied into the Darkwater suite. As soon as the door closed on the last of them, John and Jane vaulted over the railing and hurtled downward as fast as they could go.

"John Boy, that you?"

Past the third landing, John looked back to see a friendly face under a raised riot shield.

"Dooley? Wish I could stop and shoot the breeze –"

"That the Mrs.? I heard tell she was a knockout," Dooley craned over the banister to try and get a better look.

"Give Miss Peg a kiss for me," John peered up through the gloom from several floors below. A shot rang out and he hastily withdrew.

Dooley straightened up to confront the shooter, a street-tough Columbian in his rock-ribbed thirties. "I don't remember hearing anyone say 'Halt or I'll shoot.'"

"Out of my way, old-timer."

"Do you have any idea who you're fucking with?"

"All I know is a dude back there said the dude down there is worth a million bucks." The youngster tried to muscle past all 250 lbs of Dooley, who calmly stuck out a drill sergeant's foot. The shooter surfed to the next landing on his face.

"I meant me, Junior. Show a little respect. That dude down there is the reason my kids didn't grow up to be orphans. And you don't want to be pointing that thing at me, son," Dooley said to the shooter, who was spitting blood and aiming in the wrong direction. "Cause you and your kids will be thanking *me* some day." His words were validated by a flurry of gunshots and a couple of screams. He pulled a packet of beef jerky out of his flak jacket and held it out to the younger man as a peace offering. "'Course if they was bad hurt, you wouldn't hear a thing."

John and Jane had reached the bottom and an inflection point. No more stairs. Two doors.

"Lobby," Jane said. "Windows, wide open spaces, civilians."

"Garage," John said. "Underground, cover, getaway cars."

"Camera," Jane pointed.

"Christ," John said, and promptly shot out the lens. "We're probably ahead of them, but let's take it easy. Stand back." He opened the heavy door slowly, waved the Glock in the opening. Nothing. "I'll go first."

"We could go together."

The door on the landing above clanked open softly. Jane squeezed off a round. The door clanged shut. "Okay, okay, after you."

With his back against the wall and Jane behind him, John opened the door with one hand, flung it wide and dove down a ramp toward the nearest object – a large, square pillar. Seeing nothing in the way of movement and hearing no hail of gunfire, Jane somersaulted down the ramp after him. The parking garage stretched out for almost an acre in all directions, but a low ceiling gave the place a close oppressive air that was not alleviated by bright white paint or too many fluorescent bulbs, buzzing overhead like deranged hornets. Crouched beside a van in the handicapped section, they assessed the situation. One hundred yards to the exit, which was obstructed by a rolling metal grille and an automated barrier arm. No sign of any Darkwater troops. The lot was full, so they would have cover most of the way. A lone pedestrian stood waiting for the building elevator.

Bent double, they sprinted for the sunshine. The only thing between them and freedom was the metal curtain, through which they could see a sidewalk, the street, traffic, an alley near at hand. A truck double-parked next to a fire hydrant right outside. "Terminator Pest Control," it said. "What's Bugging You?"

"This baby is not moving," John decided, after heaving at the grille a time or two.

"There must be a switch," Jane put out her hand to open a yellow electrical box on the wall to the left of the grille.

"Jane!" a woman hissed from the window of the truck. It was Whitney, in a white coverall and a shower hat.

Jane felt the bullet glance off the electrical box before she heard the report from the assault rifle that fired it. The last thing she saw before she hit the concrete was Whitney holding up her cell phone. Call me, she mouthed. Seeing Jane was unhurt, John vaulted a waist-high concrete barrier and methodically squeezed off a round every time a black helmet broke the line of sight. Jane rolled behind another pillar and stood up. Darkwater soldiers were jumping off the ramp, crouching in the elevator, lining up outside the grille.

Jane locked the M4 in semi-automatic, peeled a flash grenade off her ammo belt, and nodded to John.

"This is going to be a blast."

"Pineapple in the side pocket?" John suggested.

She let fly toward the elevator, yelling "Grenade!" and spraying the area with about a third of her clip. As the mercks scattered, she made it to John's side of the barrier.

"Hon," Jane said, pulling another pin, on a concussion grenade this time. "If you want to go ahead and get the car, I'll be right with you."

36 BLOW IT UP

Upstairs in the Darkwater interrogation room, the fact that he was alive and had been freed in very short order did not soften James's mood. On the contrary, he was rapidly approaching full psychopath mode. A quick review of events confirmed that the isolated John-Jane problem had grown to include an extended family of rogue operatives. A single questionable node had become a dyad-hub with links leading to an entire resistance network of unknown dimensions and unlimited threat potential. Moreover, given his former association with Jane, an epic fail in the current context would call his own role and loyalties into question.

Accordingly, when a merck unit swarmed back in to report, James minced no words.

"Looks like we have them trapped in the parking deck, sir."

"Phasers on obliterate," James barked. "Don't bring anything back but their fucking thongs."

"Copy that." The unit vanished.

"Sergeant! Sergeant!" James thundered down the hallway. Arriving at the control center, he found a windowless, dripping mess of smoking instrument panels, cracked computer screens, and fire extinguisher foam. Sergeant Ernie was just buckling his belt and zipping his fly.

"Yessir!" he snapped a salute.

"I have a noon appointment I cannot miss. I am leaving you in charge."

"Yessir."

"If they make it to Level 3, if they get anywhere near the ring, I want you to initiate Operation Dark Crystal."

"Sir?"

"You heard me, soldier."

"Sir, with respect, ODC was defunded and decommissioned in '05. We just got word last week to resurrect. And you can see my controls are blown to kingdom come. Operation doubtful on two counts. Plus if we have men in pursuit, there's no guarantee I can pull them back in time."

"What are we talking about? Fifty men? A hundred?"

"Homeland Security contracted for ten back-up units. So we're right at fifty, sir."

James bowed his head as if deep in thought or observing a moment of silence for those not yet fallen.

"Brave lads. The order stands. Carry on."

From somewhere in the bowels of the building came a boom and a brief shudder, but James merely straightened his tie, smoothed his hair, and grabbed his overcoat on his way out. He took the stairs two at a time to meet the helicopter that was cooling its rotors on the rooftop. Before he was even buckled in, the chopper juddered skyward, hovered briefly as though basking in the midday sun, then swooped ponderously north toward Capitol Hill, like a condor scenting carrion.

In the control center, a stunned Sergeant Ernie sat down in a semi-destroyed rolling chair and surveyed the wreckage before and around him. Nothing worked. He was getting no external feed, cameras or otherwise. His terminals were dead, his servers and Wi-Fi blown to bits. It was doubtful the ODC equipment had survived intact, which was all to the good as far as he was concerned. He peered under the control console and pulled out a hidden under-desk keyboard, causing an existing keyboard to slide back out of sight. The replacement keyboard appeared to be undamaged and clicked to life when Sergeant Ernie unlocked it with a few keystrokes. He rolled backward to break the security seal on a steel credenza, exposing a standalone computer system that seemed to have suffered little more than a cracked monitor. He flipped a few switches, rolled back to type in a few command lines and waited. Almost immediately, a sexy voice said:

"Operation Dark Crystal. You are about to destroy up to 8 square miles of public-private property and up to 60,000 human lives. Is this a drill?"

Ernie snorted in consternation, like a disgruntled bull. He looked back at the monitor, which displayed a glowing aerial map of east Arlington, including Crystal City and the Pentagon. He stretched his hand toward the keyboard. Drew it back. Rolled sideways to check a terminal that was flipping in and out. Still handcuffed and trailing his pants like clouds of glory, a mildly soused Glenn Dreck wandered in from the break room, where he had been sitting all this time. In his own special darkness.

"Guess I can come out now. Was that fun or what? Say, those were some babes. Real eye candy. One of them gave me her phone number." He waved one of his business cards, on the back of which someone had scrawled '1-800-FUC-KYOU.' He was having a hard time making out the message, so he sat down to examine it more closely.

"Delta Mickey Foxtrot," Ernie breathed in horror. "Tell me you're not sitting on that keyboard?"

"Keyboard? What keyboard?" Dreck stood up and turned around.

"Thank you," the computer whispered. "Sequence engaged."

37 SHUT UP AND DRIVE

Jane sprinted down the naked length of ramp that led to Level 2, hugging the wall. The concussive force of the blast, when it came, shoved her forward, hard, like a giant invisible hand. She lurched, almost lost her footing, recovered. A flaming fender landed a little too close for comfort. At the bottom, she broke left and dodged to the rear of the ramp to get the drop on any soldiers in hot pursuit. Still trotting and ducking, she was thrown a little by the change in landscape. The low, claustrophobic upper level had given way to a vast echoing chamber, still painted bright white and garishly lit, but with fewer consumer autos and an astonishing array of military vehicles and heavy weapons. "If the one with the most toys wins," she thought, "these guys are definitely in the running."

She almost ran past John, who was standing between a tank and a really big, really black SUV, a motionless body splayed at his feet and what looked like some sort of Gameboy controller in his hand. One door of the SUV stood open.

"You've been busy," Jane noted approvingly. Then she looked more closely, and asked accusingly, "Oh wait. Did you punch Moby out?"

"Would Moby wear those shoes? DARPA dork. Tried to volunteer me for a weapons test. So I knocked him down and took his football. How about you?" John teased. "All that from one little grenade?"

"Somebody was nice enough to leave a Ford Pinto sitting around. Shit!" Jane jumped, whirled, and came down in a crouch, face to face

135

with a small tank-like robot.   As startled as she, the warbot quickly withdrew the muzzle of the M249 it had used to poke her, backed away bashfully, then rolled to her side with a nuzzling motion. "Shoo! Go away!"

"He followed me home, mom. Can I keep him?" John played with the controller, making the robot run circles around Jane.

"Cute. Didn't anyone ever tell you not to play with guns?"

John reached down to quick-release the M249 and sighed. "Once upon a time women liked appliances with lots of attachments."

"Can we discuss this in the Humvee?" Troops were by now streaming down the ramp, puddling at the bottom to do recon, and then filtering in well-coordinated teams across the entire expanse of Level 2. You could see them coming, like so many bi-pedal army ants. Jane jumped in the driver's side and clambered into the back. The warbot rolled forward expectantly.

"Better scoot now, little buddy," John said, tossing the controller and the gun into the car and climbing into the driver's seat. "Before you get hurt," he added and slammed the door.

The warbot scuttled to one side. Its camera box and bomb disposal pincers drooped. Possibly it lapsed into sleep mode. But to human eyes it looked dejected and forlorn.

The keys were in the ignition.   John studied the dashboard. "Humvee?" he chided. Reaching out tentatively he pressed a button. Bolts in all the car doors instantly shot into place. "We don't need no stinkin' Humvee." Bullets were beginning to bounce off the car, fore and aft, but with so much computer gadgetry to deal with, John was having a hard time getting the car to reverse. "THIS," he recited in the dulcet tones of a voiceover artist, "is a one-of-a-kind, ultra-luxurious, handcrafted, fully armored Conquest Knight XV. The XV stands for Extreme Vehicle. You are sitting in 6 tons of V10-powered ballistic grade aluminum and ceramic reinforced high strength steel plate built to withstand bullets, car bombs, and the odd rocket propelled grenade. All leather interior. GPS, Bluetooth, Wifi enabled. Night-vision cameras for and aft. Roof-mounted machine gun optional. Even runs on bio-fuel. What the well-dressed doomsday designer is wearing this season."

"And we know this because?"

Having managed to back the XV out of its parking slot, John attempted to steer for the exit ramp, but the little warbot was in the way, frantically to-ing and fro-ing and waving its pincers as though it had lost its artificial mind. The bullets were pinging off like BBs.

John grinned. "Common knowledge. I keep up. Danger Room. Cryptome. What do you do when you're online anyway? Sorry, little dude," he said ruefully. He was preparing to steer straight over the warbot when up ahead his path was ferociously, thunderously blocked from right and left by two enormous six-wheeled unmanned Crusher combat vehicles, one of which effortlessly demolished a parked car or two in its haste to cut John off at the pass. The Darkwater troops had pulled back. Jane peered over John's shoulder.

"Looks like DARPA Dork went home and told his daddy." It was true. Dr. Strangelove no longer graced the concrete with his inert dweeby presence. At any rate, he was nowhere to be seen.

"Man, I knew I should have hit him harder."

"No good deed goes unpunished," Jane agreed. The goggling sensors on the Crushers glared with a feral yellow light as they slowly leveled their multi-barreled high-impact weaponry at the XV. "Just how armor-plated is this thing?" Jane asked uneasily, patting her breast pocket and the Jolly Roger keychain. "'Cause charm or no charm, I'm not feeling all that lucky today, John." Lasers danced on the shiny black hood of the XV.

"Yeah. Me either."

He gunned the car into reverse. The Crushers fired at cross trajectories, doing impressive damage to an innocent herd of howitzers and an unsuspecting Abrams tank. John raced backward as more grenades exploded close enough to make the XV shudder. Braking sharply, John heeled the XV into a cross lane.

"We can outrun them, right?" Jane asked. She was sitting backward, but placed where she could both see John's face and keep track of the mercks, who were once more seeping toward them, though at a respectful distance.

"Maybe. Probably. If I can figure out how to put this thing in manual. Right now it's on autopilot and it's fighting back. Like ET it just wants to go home."

"So let it. Balls to the walls. Unless you prefer being wasted away here in Mortar-itaville."

John considered. "Oh right. They've only got a few tons on us. Apiece. I'll just tip my hat and - by the way. Where are they?"

As he spoke, two things happened. The on-board sensors went apeshit, indicating an imminent proximity threat; and, with a thunderous crash, one of the Crushers dove at them over a mountainous pile of heavy-duty tires. John stood on the gas and the XV surged forward like a herd of elephants. A herd of obese, arthritic, geriatric elephants. Nonetheless, any forward momentum was opportune because the second Crusher chose that precise moment to plow in from behind, simultaneously aiding John's balky departure and filling the void left by the XV. Just in time to cushion Crusher No. 1's crash landing.

The fleeing XV cornered abruptly enough to clip a couple of amphibious assault vehicles. The dashboard began to chime and a professionally pleasant voice filled the XV.

"This is Onstar. You appear to have suffered a collision of some kind. None of your party was wearing seatbelts. Do you require assistance?"

"Lady," John said, mashing the accelerator with all his might and reaching a whopping 20 mph, "you have no idea."

"I can see you are experiencing ignition-blocking. I can help you with that."

John and Jane exchanged glances of disbelief. The car shot forward, more or less pursued by both Crushers. I say 'more or less' because the navigation system of one of the Crushers had been damaged by the previous round of horseplay and now they were behaving like giant bumper cars, bashing into one another and jockeying for position rather than cooperating to complete the kill.

"Which way?" John asked, taking evasive action as one Crusher took a ponderous flying leap off the other one.

"Follow the yellow brick road?" Jane pointed to the yellow line stretching the length of the garage and leading in the direction from which they had originally come.

"You know, this is my third escape in two days and, don't take this personally, but I've noticed you ladies are a bit sketchy in the detail department?"

"You're doing a pre-mortem post-mortem?" Jane said, incredulous.

"Just a little constructive feedback."

"What happened to the guy who wanted me to be more spontaneous?"

"He's out looking for the lady who used to have her shit together."

The car died again. In merck territory this time. From every side, Darkwater troops began to use the run-flat tires for target practice.

"John dear," Jane said with saccharine sweetness, reaching for the M249, "why don't you take this and see if you can find something useful to do with it."

"Jane darling," John said, matching her tone, "why do I always get the girl gun?"

Possibly because they were out of grenade rounds, possibly because their AI modules prompted them to blend in with their human allies and environment, the Crushers switched to machine gun mode and began to fire indiscriminately. A merck or two went down. The dashboard began to chime again.

"Hello, this is Onstar again. I see you're still experiencing ignition blocking. Perhaps your driver would consider buckling his seatbelt?"

Red-faced but near desperate, John did as recommended. Silently, powerfully, the car throbbed fully to life. Computer screens glowed blue and green. Internal and external mirrors adjusted themselves. A mad guitar riff ignited a drum machine and music flooded the XV:

'Cause its 0 to 60 in 3.5
Baby you got the keys
Now shut up and drive, drive, drive

John burned rubber in the direction of the exit ramp. Where the yellow line split and he was getting ready to take the XV hard to the right back up the ramp toward Level 1, a large and shadowy canine shape bounded in front of the car.

"Jesus!" John swore, and heeled hard to the left instead. "Did I hit it?" Before Jane could answer, the vehicle lifted off one wheel as one of the Crushers loosed a last grenade and atomized a nearby pillar.

"More good news," Jane warned from the back, as an MRAP with a gun mount careened out of hiding on the exit ramp and made a beeline for their tail. "APC on your six. Oh, and Dorkmobiles at 9 o'clock." The Crushers were rolling their way at top speed and in tandem.

"And a wall at 3. Alrighty then," John said, gripping the steering wheel, "let's try high noon."

Straddling the left branch of the yellow line, they were rapidly approaching the gaping black mouth of what appeared to be a tunnel. A ten-foot tall chain-link gate blocked entry and in the middle of that gate was a sign: "DANGER RESTRICTED AREA HIGH VOLTAGE"

"Damn it's that dog again." John swerved as something on four feet leaped in front of the fence.

"Don't look now, but that 'dog' is shooting at us," Jane pointed out. The creature challenging them was no flesh and blood K9 SWAT team member, no combat-trained German Shepherd or Labrador, but a military dogbot, essentially a steel frame riveted to uncanny mechanical legs, with a gun for a body, and no head. It crouched before the gate and laid down enough fire to stop anything on two feet. The bullets raised a few sparks, but otherwise the XV was unfazed. This time John did not slow down.   He just switched on his high beams and, if anything, accelerated.

"OK, Rin Tin Tin.   This is an intelligence test."

38 DEAD END STREET

At the last possible moment the dogbot sprang aside, the gate snapped off its hinges in a fountain of blue sparks, and the XV went barreling through the trapezoid opening into pitch darkness. As the tunnel swallowed them, Jane clambered into the front passenger seat and pressed the Home symbol on the computer display.

"Uh, I was planning on using that," John said as the night vision screen flipped back to the main menu. The headlights illuminated a long curving corridor of rough-hewn stone wide enough for two 18-wheelers to drive abreast. Carefully. To the left and right, closed metal doors or open passageways appeared at intervals. So far they were travelling solo. Apparently the Crushers could not distinguish friend from foe, which was buying them a little time.

"What we could really use is reinforcements." Jane tapped the phone option and entered Whitney's number on the touch screen keypad. When the phone began to ring, she tapped the screen again and put it back in night vision mode. "Don't know about you," she admitted grimly, "but I'm down to one clip."

"Same, plus the girl gun."

"And - a paintball grenade," Jane said, tossing it in the air. "Apparently Junior likes to play soldier in his off hours. He's got a whole duffle bag of tricks back there. C'mon Whitney." The phone kept ringing.

"Won't work underground anyway, sweetcakes." John saw headlights in the rearview for the first time. One set, then two. Suddenly the XV flashed through a circular chamber lined with old M35 supply trucks. Yellow hazard signs streamed by: DANGER! EXPLOSIVES. There was a slight dip, a pronounced rise, and the XV was tooling down a wider section of tunnel where the ceiling was propped up at intervals by massive stone supports. "No signal."

"Jane," Whitney's voice crackled through. "Jane, whatever you do, DON'T come out."

Jane turned to John and rolled her eyes. "Can't come out, can't stay in. Are you saying we should just sit back and embrace the suck?"

"It's an NRA convention out here. But there are alternative exits if you can get down to the next level and access the tunnel system. Do you read?"

"Roger that, Henny Penny. Tunnel system accessed."

"Who knew there was a tunnel system?" John asked. Jane motioned for silence.

"Listen. I'm going to give you some numbers.   3E6377, 3W5456, 3E1313..."

The phone died.

"Oh great. GPS coordinates?" Jane punched the Navigation button, which read out their last location in decimal format: 38.851403, -77.050689. John slowed down and aimed the headlights at a doorway. Stenciled numbers glowed in neon colors: 3W6020.

"Street address." He rolled to the next passage, where the numbers read: 3E5999. "Descending. We missed the first one. That leaves –"

"5456 and 1313. So much for running on night vision, we'll need the lights – "

"Sweet Jesus!" John interrupted her. The XV slammed sideways as an up-armored Humvee shot out of the passage like a guided missile, smashing head on into the XV and trying to pin it to the opposite wall.

For a minute the two vehicles did a sort of grinding paso doble, circling wheel to wheel, tires smoking. As John struggled to break free and get the car pointed in the right direction, Jane lurched into the back, almost falling to the floor and pulling the pin on the paint grenade as she went. Steadying herself on one of the seats, she hit the sunroof button and, quick as a prairie dog, popped up through the narrow opening. Like a goddess armed with a thunderbolt, she reared back and hurled the grapefruit-sized paint-balloon with all her might. She waited just long enough to see the unusually viscous pink paint explode across the Humvee windshield before dropping back inside.

It wasn't much. But it was enough.

The paint-blinded Humvee veered into a phalanx of gas cylinders shackled to the tunnel walls. The cylinders broke from their chains, scattering like gigantic bowling pins. Several lost their valves at impact and began to rocket from surface to surface, propelled by the highly pressurized escaping gas. One punched through the hood of the Humvee, where the hot engine ignited the remaining gas in the cylinder with a hearty KABOOM. Another chased Jane and John down the tunnel like a thing possessed, now behind them, now before them, now frisking along side like a dolphin at play. By the time it sputtered to a clangorous rest, and they could slow down to check the numbers, they were already in the 2000 block. Dense smoke billowed ominously, menacingly, in their wake. In front of them the darkness seemed to grow darker and to reach out with a million ghostly fingers. Literally. Dangling wires brushed the windshield and tickled the roof of the car. Craning forward over the steering wheel, John whistled softly.

"Silly string or fuse cord?"

"I'd go with 'Controlled Demolition' for $1,000, but I keep thinking any minute now we may run out of road or wind up right back where we started. Incidentally? That was 1317," Jane pointed.

"I see it. 1315 coming up. I, on the other hand, keep wondering why in the world - "

"Nobody's caught up with us yet?" Jane peered uneasily out the back, where the rear window was a mass of starbursts.

"Or met us coming the other way."

144

Right on cue, myriad headlights of multiple vehicles bobbed into view from both directions.

"Holy –" Jane said.

"Fucking –" John said.

"SHIT!!" they yelled in unison. John gunned it to the next cross tunnel and parallel parked, totally blocking access from all other sides with the bulky XV. He set the parking brake with a jerk, unbuckled his seat belt, and grabbed the girl gun.

"Uh, what are you doing?" Jane asked, a tad strained.

"What are *you* doing? Let's boogie."

"There's no number."

"85% of buildings don't have a 13th floor. 1313. Duh." Jane raised her eyebrows. "Triskaidekaphile. Born on the 13th. Turned 13 on Friday the 13th. Met you -"

"On the 12th."

"But made love just after midnight on the 13th." The merck headlights were rapidly closing in. "Jane," John said, in the upward sliding tone of one who was being goaded past his limit.

"John," Jane harmonized, mulishly.

"This time," John insisted, holding out his hand, "we get on the train together."

Bowing to the paucity of options, Jane grabbed her gun and his hand as half a dozen MRAPs and Humvees screeched to a halt, training their headlights on the XV and blocking escape from three sides. Dozens of soldiers bailed out and got into position, targeting the XV and preparing for a final shootout. Hoping to buy some time, John tripped the locks on the XV. Enough light bled through from the main tunnel to show that he and Jane stood at the foot of a few uneven steps leading to an otherwise unlit and extremely compact corridor. Acrid smoke stung their eyes and burned their lungs. Beyond the steps, the corridor sloped gently upward. With the XV for the moment providing an effective barricade, they felt their way forward with tense rapidity, searching for ledges, holes, or drop-offs, unsure when or if bullets would follow.

"Boy, this better be the beginning of a beautiful friendship or you are never going to hear the end of it," Jane swore.

"Darlin', if I'm wrong, I expect to be eternally sorry, believe me."

"What gets me is I'm probably about to die and all I got was a lousy keychain."

"Just so you know," John said, a little hurt by her tone, "That ain't no crackerjack prize."

"I meant I don't know why. Cosmically speaking," Jane explained.

"That lousy keychain is why. Existentially speaking."

"Over and above the sentimental value?"

"Try over and above a year's pay. And – oh yeah - the future of the free world."

Down below the mercks had grown bolder. Concluding that their body armor was fairly reliable and the Does' ammo situation was fairly dire, they plastered themselves over every inch of the Knight XV, aggressively seeking a means of getting around, over, or through. One bright boy lay down on top of the car and, thrusting one arm awkwardly into the void, managed to toss a flare up the tunnel. Due to the slight incline, the flare rolled harmlessly down again, leaving John and Jane safely in shadow, but perfectly illuminating the young man.

"How did you get to be such a big boy?" Jane wondered. "For heaven's sake. A bunch of weekend warriors, kids, and your pal Dooley?"

"They," John agreed, "are not the enemy. Now where the hell is that exit."

The corridor leveled off and seemed to open up into an alcove or small chamber. Jane went a little too sharply to her right.

"Ow," she said, rubbing her forehead. "Not here. Dead end."

"Would you care to re-phrase that? But seriously, there must be a door, a hatchway, a duct opening."

Down below, they could hear the soldiers talking. An effort was being made to push or pull the Knight XV out of the way, to no avail.

"Where are them damn Crushers when you need 'em?"

"A little IED under the rear axle would solve all our problems."

"IED? Really, fuckchop? Well, just feel free to help yourself. See that black plastic liner up there? It's not exactly bubblewrap."

"Line up, you sorry bunch of fobbits," a senior merck barked. "Iraq rules. Body count equals bonuses. Two million split 40 ways. Easiest damn money you'll ever put in your pockets. Or a hooker's g-string."

"No hurry, they ain't goin' nowhere." There was an eloquent pause during which someone was heard to hawk and spit derisively. "Like shootin' womp rats in Beggar's Canyon."

There was a door. John and Jane found it with very little trouble in the very middle of the rear wall. Just a simple metal door like all the others in the main tunnel, with exposed hinges and an ordinary round doorknob. It was locked, however, and there appeared to be no way to open it. John was twisting the knob and pulling hard, with one foot against the doorjamb, when Jane gasped and jerked him to one side. Red gunsight lasers burned through the darkness, painting the area where John had just been standing. The mercks, detecting the slightest hint of movement, yelled from they were lying atop the XV and let loose a merciless barrage. Bullets ripped the air, chiseled stone from the walls, flattened or burst against the metal door, ricocheted in every direction, including back at the shooters, who assumed that John and Jane were returning fire and hammered away harder than ever.

Although they were about to be cut to ribbons, Jane and John seemed to be slow dancing, molded together, turning this way and that in the farthest corner at the corridor's end. In fact, John was trying to shield

Jane with his body and she was resisting with every fiber of her being.

"Dammit, John!"

"The keychain," he tried to make himself understood over the tumult. "Jen."

"You bastard!" Jane raged and stomped his instep.

"Ow! Don't be an idiot. Listen. Iceland."

"You think I won't hop the next bullet out of here?" she screamed, tears of rage streaming down her cheeks. "You think I want to live forever?"

For answer, John lifted her off her feet and pressed her into the protective angle formed by the two walls, pretending not to feel the bullet that ripped his pants and grazed his thigh. "Kiss me," he demanded. "Like it's the last time."

39 END OF THE WORLD AS WE KNOW IT

They heard the siren whooping before they felt the bullets cease. Red strobe lights were flashing in the main tunnel when they opened their eyes and came up for air. Down below the mercks were yelling at the tops of their lungs:

"Fire in the hole. FIRE IN THE HOLE!"

The mercks were packing it in and bugging out at top speed. Over the sirens and the strobe lights their unit leaders were yelling, "Go, go, go!" They piled into their rigs, put the pedal to the metal, and were almost instantly gone like so many bats out of hell. The sirens stopped but the strobe lights kept silently, eerily flashing.

"Taking a poll here, " John said, feeling instinctively for the XV keys. "Why do you suppose those guys cut and run –"

"Just as they were about to annihilate our million dollar asses?"

The strobe lights faded to black just then, leaving John and Jane in total eclipse.

"About this good luck charm - " Jane began.

"Shhh," John reached for the girl gun, which he had dropped at the height of the fray. Behind them the door was opening slowly, slowly, slowly. They moved stealthily out of the line of sight and stopped breathing. A thin white blade pierced the darkness, lengthened, strengthened, grew into an arc of incandescence that swept toward them, the area of illumination increasing as a familiar male voice asked the age-old question:

"So – how many mercenaries does it take to screw in a light bulb?"

"As many as we fucking say so," John said, hustling Jane through the door and into a major league HVAC room, full of pumps, pipes, gauges, and compressors. "Oh wait – is this a no-bid government contract?"

"If you have to ask," Jane blew Vinnie an air-kiss, "you probably can't afford it."

Having ascertained that there were no mercks to deal with and no signs of pursuit, Vinnie slammed the door and ran to catch up. "I was gonna say 'Kill 'em all and let God sort it out.' But looks like you guys beat me to it."

"But we're still looking at a forecast of Hiroshima with a chance of Armageddon. Now," John stressed, taking the grey-painted aluminum stairs two at a time. He threw open the door at the top and found himself facing - a bright blue curtain spangled with glittering stars. Vinnie shoved the handgun he was carrying inside his white exterminator's jumpsuit and reached around Jane to pick up a silver insecticide sprayer.

"Got cooties?" he teased.

"Oh look," Jane retorted, as they drew back the curtain and stepped into a fabulous toy store, "if it isn't Peter Pan."

"Uh – kids? We need to get lost before we get found. Or worse," John said, ejecting the clip from the girl gun and clearing the chamber. A bin of plastic Uzis provided the perfect hiding place. Not to be outdone, Jane gifted the M4 to a larger than life-sized stuffed flamingo.

"WHAT you all think you doing?" Emerging from an aisle strewn with orange CAUTION signs, where he had been quietly mopping the floor, the elderly and slightly deaf proprietor accosted them. "Trompin' in here on my nice clean floors. Can't you read?" He pointed to a sign on the door that led out to the Crystal City underground mall: PUPPET HEAVEN: CLOSED FOR THE INAUGURATION. The metro entrance was visible from where they stood. "You go on out of here. Get along now."

They departed with alacrity, only to find themselves poised at the edge of what seemed to be a mad rush to the metro. In a one-way torrent of motion, they stood apart and alone. Well, almost. Souvenir hawkers prowled up and down the banks of the DC-bound multitude. To them, our trio stuck out like toothsome lambs separated from the tougher, hard-bitten flock. They crowded in. They besieged.

"Baby, you best cover them pretty legs. It's cold outside."

"You got to have a t-shirt. Something to show the grandchildren."

Money and goods were hurriedly exchanged and the plague of hawkers moved on.

"I gotta call the girls, who are still looking for you in all the wrong places. You gotta disappear," Vinnie said, eying the oversupply of cops in attendance.

"Like a coupla needles in a haystack," John promised, bumping fists with his pal, in keeping with the man code: 'Thou shalt not publicly display affection toward another brother.' PS - Not even when he has just saved your raggedy ass. PPS - Especially if the wife or gf is present. John cleared his throat. "We owe ya big time, bro."

"Yeah, yeah," Vinnie said, walking backward. "Thanksgiving. Your place. It's all about the stuffing. I'll send you mom's recipe."

"You got it. Right, sweetheart?"

"Mom's recipe," Jane repeated, waving gaily. "Can't wait. Of course," she confided to John as they bought their passes and headed down the escalator to queue for the next DC-bound train, " you and I both know I can't cook worth shit."

"To say nothing of our overall kitchen deficit. But I've been known to find my way around a turkey. What say we jump off that bridge when we come to it?'

"Works for me," Jane said charitably, trying to figure out how to get a pair of sweats on over her boots. "Let him dream."

She had to hurry. The train was pulling in. Since it was almost noon and the official ceremony had already begun, they were able to squeeze aboard the very last car. As they shuffled to the rear, John raised his head. He heard a familiar violin riff. The Verve? On Muzak? But no. Just down the platform two buskers had set up shop with the aforementioned violin and a cello. Their music soared over the incoherent crackling of the announcement system. John recognized the opening bars of Bittersweet Symphony:

It's a bittersweet symphony, this life
Trying to make ends meet
You're a slave to money then you die

"I can change, I can't change, I can change," Jane sang. Then the doors slid shut and the train moved on. John and Jane squeezed onto the bench seat at the very back and looked around the car. It was filled with people from every age group and almost every walk of life. Grandmothers sat with strippers, college kids listened to war vets, street punks made room for young families. John spied the little girl from the Pentagon, still clutching her origami dove. It was one of those rare moments of mass happiness. Everyone was smiling, kind, some shade of euphoric - about what you'd expect from a train full of people bound for the afterlife. Despite their 'Got Hope?' and 'Change We Can Believe In' hoodies, John and Jane presented the sole somber note, a grave and slightly blood-stained contrast to the spirit of carnival around them. As if catching their mood, the little girl looked up at her mother.

"We're too late, aren't we?"

Taking her hand and squeezing it, her mother smiled down reassuringly, "Oh now, you never know. Maybe not."

John laced Jane's fingers between his own as the train broke out of the underground into the light, flashing over the Potomac toward DC just as the ring of explosives beneath Crystal City detonated. The earth and the train moved as one for an instant. The passengers swayed against one another, knocked together, landed in strange laps, but came up laughing like kids on a roller coaster. Behind them, out the rear windows – and unobserved since all eyes were directed forward in joy and anticipation – the Crystal City skyline seemed to shudder and heave. Then the train was in the city proper and vanishing in a sea of people. Millions of people, more than the city had ever seen at any one time. Millions of people, who had journeyed thousands of miles from hundreds of places all across America to witness the crowning moment of a history they had helped to make on a single November day. And out of those happy innocent well-meaning millions exactly two had the slightest inkling that nothing was as it seemed, that the world was far different than they imagined it to be, that their future had in fact been determined elsewhere - incrementally, by a relative few, over the course of half a century - and that it awaited them now with jaws wide open.

AFTER –
ARMY OF ME

Outside the portholes of the Casablanca, the day was sharp and cold as a Viking sword. The sloop was anchored in Reykjavik's Old Harbor, tucked in between the whale-hunting and the whale-watching vessels. Snug and cozy down below, Jane and John were in conference via Skype with the ever-faithful Gerald.

"Good news, you two." On the computer screen, Gerald could be seen adding a splash of Irish whiskey to his morning coffee. "Your loans failed to materialize BUT – for reasons I am totally unable to explain or comprehend - there has been a multiplication of the ones and zeroes in your joint account and as a result I can now pronounce you financially solvent."

"Till death do us liquidate?" John quipped.

"Well at any rate till the next round of banking crises. Which I for one expect at any moment. But I have to ask you, how did you do it? I'm just dying to know."

"Interesting turn of phrase," John observed.

"We could tell you," Jane said, "but you wouldn't believe it."

"We could tell you," John said, "but if you did believe it, we'd have to kill you."

"Point taken, dear boy," Gerald waved his hand in surrender. "I worked for Enron in a previous life, so I can well imagine. Is it also taboo to ask what you will be doing with yourselves?"

"Off with his head! Off with his head!" a fourth voice joined the conversation as a brightly colored parrot landed on John's shoulder.

"Louie!" Jane said, admonishingly.

"Ah! I see, said the blind man. Going in for corrections are you?"

"Strictly upper end," Jane insisted.

"For the top 1%," John added.

"*Liberte, Egalite, Fraternite*. I follow you. Sounds like a brave new market. I can't think of any competition you're likely to encounter. On the other hand I can't begin to imagine how you'll go about building your brand."

"Well, we're going to keep the start-up pretty lean. Mostly word-of-mouth. Plain black business card, white letters –"

"Cream, angel," Jane inserted.

"With our names and the name of the company - 'Elite Solutions.'"

"And," Jane added brightly, "we do have a logo…"

And so they did. An updated pirate emblem. Sort of a Jolly Roger-U.N. mashup, with a Guy Fawkes mask set against the skeletal outlines of a gridded globe. No cross-bones. A prototype was flapping in the wind at the very top of their main-mast, above the American and Icelandic flags dictated by custom and the law of the sea. The black and white cloth had attracted the attention of a short-sighted puffin, which paused and circled a time or two, possibly drawn by a color scheme that in Puffinland shrieked 'Come Hither.' Discovering the cheat in short order and retaining a sense of injury, the bird continued on its way, winging toward Reykjavik, careening above streets, darting past bonfires and police vans, swooping over a massive assemblage of protesters who were banging pots and pans and yelling at the tops of their lungs outside the Parliament building. The noise only increased as the former Prime

Minister-cum-Central Banker emerged from a morning of hearings and deliberations. It reached such a crescendo that the already agitated puffin was thoroughly unnerved. With airspeed, altitude, and atmospheric conditions miraculously combining, the petrified bird released a full payload of guano, scoring a direct hit on the beleaguered politician, who found himself at once dripping with bird shit and facing an infinity of placards which read (in Icelandic) "Helvítis*Fokkin*Fokk" and (in English) "Just*Getting*Started."

I. C. SPRINGMAN

ABOUT THE AUTHOR

With roots in the '60's and hopes in the Occupy Movement,
I.C. Springman is an absolute nobody
who believes that an understanding of global financial arrangements
and their impact on ordinary people in every walk of life
is the first step toward altering those arrangements
for the benefit of everybody everywhere.
No matter what they tell you -
Another world is possible.

www.ingramcontent.com/pod-product-compliance
Lightning Source LLC
Chambersburg PA
CBHW070926130626
46555CB00001B/307